Still Searching

by

Lorraine Ophelia Smith

To Dr. Scott,

From one HBCU grad to another; and to my new favorite Dermatologist.

All the best,

Lorraine Smith

DORRANCE
PUBLISHING CO
EST. 1920
PITTSBURGH, PENNSYLVANIA 15238

Dorrance Publishing Co
585 Alpha Drive
Suite 103
Pittsburgh, PA 15238
Visit our website at www.dorrancebookstore.com

ISBN: 978-1-4809-5811-1
eISBN: 978-1-4809-5834-0

To my son Joshua, you are truly an amazing gift from above, and I thank God for you every day. I love you to life!

Introduction

As a teenager growing up in the traditional South during the seventies, Brenda felt like an outcast. Integration was becoming a reality, but it was difficult for people to deal with or accept change. Sure, by law, black people had more opportunities, but there was an unwritten rule of "know your place and stay in it," and, for Brenda, that meant in the home as well.

Not the prettiest or the smartest, a bit awkward, but a Southern girl with big city dreams: that was Brenda Peekson. She stood at five feet, nine inches tall with walnut colored skin, sable brown, medium length, curly hair and piercing almond shaped coffee bean eyes. Even as a young lady, her views on life were different from others in her home and community. As one of six siblings and oldest daughter with a traditional Southern mother, Brenda was raised to be a respectable and obedient girl, which meant she was taught and expected to know how to cook, wash clothes, clean, and iron.

Her brothers were treated like princes. Stephen, the favorite, had no chores; he could have friends come over and have sleepovers. He stayed up later than Brenda, even on school nights. Like the boys, Brenda was encouraged to attend college, not necessarily for career advancement, but instead to find, date, and marry a suitable college man from a good and respectable family.

In her early years, Brenda was a people pleaser, even though she was not happy. She figured if she did what she was told and went beyond the call of duty she would be loved and accepted. However, as she got older, Brenda realized that the more she did, the more she was expected to do.

More was never enough, so she decided to forget about pleasing others and concentrated on pleasing herself.

Chapter One

Growing up in the South had its moments, but was not the place to be if you wanted to live on the edge or in the fast lane. In fact, it was anything but that. Bloomington, Virginia was a town that reminds you of the sitcoms from the nineteen fifties and sixties.

We lived in what many would call an upper-middle-class neighborhood. There were playgrounds, parks, picnic areas, fine schools, and friendly neighbors who would invite you over for dinners, as well as an occasional barbecue. The men would golf, while the women swapped recipes.

Did I mention we were the only black family in the neighborhood at the time? It was fine, however, because my dad was in the oil business and we traveled throughout North America and abroad, always in the same circles. Once in a while, we would come across other black families, which was exciting, but rare.

The only time we would see black people was when there was a special event at school or when we would go to "the other side of town" to visit my grandmother.

I always looked forward to the other side of town, but not necessarily to my grandmother's house—my mother's mother. There were six children in my family. I was the second oldest child and the oldest daughter, which meant I was stuck in the middle.

I read a lot of books and poetry by black authors. I, as opposed to my siblings, always asked questions, said what was on my mind, and acted independently of everyone else.

My teachers admired and praised me for taking a stand for what I believed in, regardless of how unpopular that stand might have been. They encouraged me to consider law as a career choice.

But the atmosphere was very different at home. I could never measure up and I continually heard things like:

"Brenda, why can't you be more like your brother, Stephen? He is a good boy; he never causes any trouble, never talks back, makes good grades, he does what he is supposed to do, and, most of all, he has manners. Be seen and not heard, and last, but not least, you will never be like your brother, Stephen."

And every time my younger siblings got in trouble, of course, it was my fault. Without even being in the vicinity, I would hear:

"Brenda, you should have known better; you are the oldest!"

I would say, "I thought Stephen was the oldest. Why am I the scapegoat?"

Needless to say, I would have to go and get my own switch from the oak tree in the backyard and take a whipping, just for being the middle kid. There were times when I asked myself why I was even born?

I couldn't have many friends, and the friends I did have had to be light, bright or damn near white because that represented the good. I couldn't go many places without being supervised by my brother. Boys were out of the question. I couldn't belong to any clubs or organizations if they required meeting after school. For a teenager, this was nothing short of being in Hell. I guess my mother was trying to protect me, but her tactics left more to be desired.

Who I really enjoyed visiting was my father's mother, Grandmother Mary Ann Peekson. I could see myself in her. Grandmother Peekson was a very attractive woman with a flawless, golden complexion and long, thick, salt and pepper hair, which she usually kept in a bun. She was a tall, strong, and independent woman, who always encouraged her children and grandchildren to excel in whatever made them happy. She never degraded any of us. Her famous words were: "The sky is the limit. You can do anything. You are the best; walk with your head held high, and look people straight in the eye when you speak with them." Kids of all ages loved to come over to Granny Peekson's house because she made learning fun, always listening to what we had to say.

I always admired my grandmother. When most women her age were in rocking chairs, she was out campaigning for some cause or other, whether it was going door-to-door, making sure everyone in her community was registered to vote, helping the homeless, tutoring kids for free, or marching the streets for civil rights, not to mention her many church duties. No matter how busy she was, she would always find time for anyone who needed her.

As opposed to degrading me, Grandmother Peekson made me feel like a million bucks. The only bad thing was she lived in Reno, Nevada whereas I lived here in Virginia. We didn't get a chance to see her that often.

When it was time for me to attend college, I wanted to get as far away from home as I could. I applied to schools throughout the country, from Maine to California. I really had no interest in these schools, beyond the fact that they happened to be far away from home. Besides, my mother was bugging me to attend the local state college, which was a no-go for me.

One day, after class, my favorite high school teacher, Mrs. Richman, asked me to consider her alma mater, Edgar University in North Carolina. She said it was a good, predominantly black, private, liberal arts university. Moreover, it was far enough away, yet still rather close to home.

Mrs. Richman even offered to take me to visit the campus one weekend. I told her it sounded great, but I would have to clear it with my parents.

I went home that night after dinner and I asked my parents if I could check out Edgar University with my teacher, Mrs. Richman. Not knowing much about Edgar University, I must have given one hell of a sales pitch because they said yes.

The next morning, I saw Mrs. Richman in the parking lot and gave her the good news. We made arrangements to leave early Saturday morning and make a day of it. During those days, it was perfectly fine to go away with your teacher without worrying about being abused or kidnapped.

As promised, Mrs. Richman was at my home bright and early. After stopping for coffee and snacks, we were off. She was a cool teacher. She believed in class discussions, yet some said it was to avoid planning a daily class schedule. I didn't care; she gave her students a chance to express themselves.

As we were driving down the highway, she suggested I put on some music. As I was looking through her collection, I was shocked to discover we listen to the same soulful music. I decided to play something wild and funky. Mrs. Richman thought I had made a good choice as well because she began to drive faster, as if she didn't have a care in the world.

There was nothing ahead of us except the open road. We had a great time, talking about her college days, men, life, and her husband whom she met at Edgar University. She asked me some general questions like what I planned on majoring in and did I have any hobbies? She also wanted to know about my family, if I had a boyfriend, and so on. We were having such a good time I didn't realize we were there until I saw a sea of beautiful black people. There were students sitting on the wall playing chess and backgammon. Others watched people and cars go by, and a cool guy in shades listened to music on his boom box. I saw all sizes and shades of black people. Tall, short, cool, nerdy, and handsome ones. I felt like I had reached the Promised Land.

Mrs. Richman gave me a tour of the campus and introduced me to some faculty members who happened to be there that day. The students were personable. Everyone wore a smile and greeted me as if they knew me, or as if I were a long-lost friend. It felt like family, and I wanted to be a part of it. The campus was well kept. The lawns were greener than ole St. Patrick himself, the hedges were manicured just so, and there were huge oak and maple trees swaying in the breeze while students sat under them in the shade.

Mrs. Richman happened to have an application for Edgar University with her. She gave it to me and I filled it out. On our way back to Bloomington, I couldn't stop talking about Edgar University. I fell in love with that school. It was like I was under a spell. When we arrived at home, Mrs. Richman and I went into the living room where my mom was knitting a sweater for, guess who, my brother. I told her how excited I was about attending that fall. My mother basically ignored me and thanked Mrs. Richman for taking me out for the day. She showed her to the door and said goodnight.

After Mrs. Richman left, my mom told me I was going to the same school Stephen attended so he could keep an eye on me. Then when it was time for me to go to college, I refused to attend the same university as him for obvious reasons. With the support of my father, I got my wish. I needed to get away and find myself.

Finally, on August 26, 1978, I, a seventeen-year-old, independent young lady, was on her way to college. I was on my own and ready to tackle the world, as well as to meet new people, especially men.

In high school, I didn't even date or go to the prom, but regardless, I packed up the car and kissed everyone goodbye. I was off in my convertible, with the wind racing through my hair and with my music on the highest volume. I was filled with every emotion imaginable: excitement, fear, uncertainty, joy, and a true sense of reality. *This is it girl*, I said to myself, *you wanted independence and freedom, well you got it, Ms. Thang.*

Edgar University was a school that treated everyone as an equal. No one was better than anyone else. The fact that Edgar was located in the heart of the city didn't hurt either. Coming from a small town in Virginia, the most exciting thing was the annual county fair.

Not knowing what to expect, I arrived on campus with my assignments stating, "Please report to Adams Hall upon your arrival to Edgar University." I thought I would report to the dormitory, get my keys, and pay whatever fees necessary. However, when I arrived to the dorm, the lines of students waiting to get room assignments stretched for miles. Not being any different, I took my place in line. I engaged in idle chitchat with other students.

"Hi, my name is Brenda Peekson. I'm from Bloomington, Virginia. How are you? What's your name? Where are you from? It certainly is hot out here in the sun."

The next thing I knew, I was at the front of the line getting my room assignment, along with other information I would soon need, like where to go next. I arrived at my room. It was nothing special, by any means. It was just two twin beds, two desks, dresser drawers, and a wall mirror. I was the first to arrive, so I claimed my space and rushed off to the financial and registration buildings, where I met more lines of people. It wasn't bad, however, because everyone, in general, was kind.

I guess the administration felt sorry for us green freshmen and decided we could register for classes the following day. Thus, I returned to my room to unpack, relax, and get settled. Then after taking a shower and a nap, I decided to explore the campus.

It was considered "Freshmen Week," which meant there were only freshmen and football players on campus. Not much to choose from, but that was okay. I really needed to take this time to get familiar with the campus and the surrounding area. And, besides, I was waiting for those distinguished upperclassmen.

The next morning, I got up at dawn, showered, and raced off to register for my classes. While waiting in line, I noticed a tall, dark, athletic-type man standing by an oak tree like a lion watching and waiting on his prey. Probably saying to himself, "New meat." At that moment, he strolled over to me and said, "Hello there, I was just noticing you from afar. You are truly a beautiful young lady. Oh, excuse me. My name is Alfred Holmes. I'm a senior, majoring in chemical engineering here at Edgar. Once you finish registering, would you like to go out for something cold to drink?"

"Sure, that would be nice, but wouldn't you like to know my name first?" I asked.

"Not now. Tell me all about yourself over drinks. Let's say Melba's Coffee Shop around 3:30. Is that okay with you?"

"That sounds great, but where is Melba's?" I replied.

"It's just a block away from campus. You can't miss it."

"I'll see you there."

Just then, a fellow female student walked up to me and said, "Girl, please be careful. Alfred Holmes is a womanizing, cheating dog who can't even graduate from college. He doesn't think with his head. Not the one between his shoulders anyway. From one sister to another, watch yourself."

"Thank you for the advice. I will be careful," I said. *She's probably jealous and wants him for herself, or maybe he rejected her in the past,* I thought.

Finally, after registering for my last class, I dashed to my dorm to freshen up and change into something more feminine, like a sundress. I arrived at Melba's Coffee House at 3:25 in the afternoon, and Alfred was seated in a booth, sipping on a frosted mug. He had changed his clothes as well. He wore a crisp, white collar shirt opened enough to see his forest-like chest. His jeans looked as if they were made just for him, clinging to his body like a glove on a hand. The sun glanced over his bronzed, sculptured body with small beads of sweat rolling down his chest like a stream of water rolling down the side of a huge mountain. He made my heart, as well as other parts of my body I didn't know existed, skip a beat.

Alfred noticed me at the door and motioned me to come over.

"Hi, Alfred, it's nice to see you again," I said.

"It's nice to see you as well. You look even lovelier than you did earlier."

"Well, thank you, Alfred," I replied.

As the waitress came over, he asked, "What would you like to drink, Ms.?"

"An iced tea, please with a glass of water, thank you," I answered.

"You are so polite; you must be a Southern lady."

"You are correct."

"Now you know my name, what might yours be, Miss.?"

"My name is Brenda Peekson."

"Brenda, that's a nice name. Tell me about yourself and why you decided to attend Edgar University out of all the colleges and universities in America?"

"What is this? An interview?"

"It may sound like it, but this is no interview."

"Okay, I'll tell you if you will promise to do the same."

"You have a deal."

"I am seventeen years old and I come from a small town in Virginia. I'm the second oldest in a family of six children, three girls and three boys. My dad is the director of operations for a major oil company, and my mother is a housewife. I have traveled all over North America, as well as parts of Europe. I plan to major in marketing/advertising. I enjoy cooking, writing, reading, trying new things, football, basketball, arts and crafts, meeting people, as well as organizing and planning functions." I went on, "I came to Edgar University because I wanted to get away from my home setting, claim my independence, and be all I can on my own. I also wanted to attend a black college because I've only attended predominately white schools. .."

Alfred looked impressed, which was good because I didn't want him to think I was some naïve girl who wasn't well-rounded.

"Alfred, now it's your turn."

"Well, you know my name. I'm from Iowa, Des Moines. Yes, there are black people in Iowa."

"I know that, Alfred. Remember, I'm the world traveler here," I told him.

"Okay. I am the oldest of three children. My father is a truck driver, and my mom is a postal worker. My family looks up to me. I'm the first to go to college. I feel if I don't succeed, my family will be very disappointed. I have been at Edgar for four years, majoring in chemical engineering. I have a part-time job at a chemical plant in town to help pay for my education. I also enjoy reading, sports, and meeting people."

"Why is a man such as yourself interested in me? Are you just out to score another 'notch in your belt,' shall we say?"

"During this conversation, have I given you the slightest impression I want to go to bed with you?"

"No, you haven't, and you seem to be a sincere person, but you must also see things from my point of view. And, besides, after you left today, a woman came up to me and said to be wary of you because you're a cheating dog. So, naturally, my guard is up."

"Brenda, please judge me for me, and not from what you hear other people say about me."

"You're right. I am sorry. I shouldn't prejudge you, or rely purely on hearsay."

"Apology accepted."

At that moment, I realized I had found a true friend in Alfred.

During the following weeks, Alfred and I were inseparable. He took me by the hand and showed me around campus, and informed me of the do's and don'ts. Needless to say, I was the envy of every girl on campus. In passing, I would hear things, such as:

"Why is he with her, a green freshman? What does she have?"

"Alfred is just going to get all the sex and money he can get out of Brenda and then leave her ass."

I just ignored their comments because I knew the real Alfred. He took me everywhere. He told me where to get the best deals on used books, which classes to take, and which professors to avoid. He also showed me where to shop, get my hair done, and where to get great take-out. We went to museums, parks, grocery stores, and shopping malls, among other places.

Alfred was a loner, because most of his friends had already graduated. I was the new kid on the block who needed guidance and wisdom. Alfred, like most men, was the type who needed to feel wanted and appreciated. And since I had never really experienced such one-on-one attention, I welcomed Alfred's devotion.

One Sunday morning, I attended the campus church with some other girls from the dorm. The church reminded me of my church at home. It was large, with many stained-glass windows, as well as pews that could fit a small town comfortably. The atmosphere was filled with the spirit of Jesus. The choirs were dressed in red and white robes, singing the gospel so intensely that people began feeling the spirit and testifying. And the Reverend Mark Hynes was just as vocal. Reverend Hynes was very tall, dark, and a bit intense. He wasn't the kind of man you would want to upset. If you were sinning, he made you rethink your ways. Reverend Hynes scared everyone straight. God was truly speaking through him.

After receiving my spiritual uplift, I went back to my room to find a young lady in her bra and panties, blasting the radio, while dancing provocatively.

She was my roommate, Sheila Norma Gadson, from New York City. Sheila was a manly type of woman, with a front gold tooth. She loved to party, meet guys, have sex, and hang out. This meant she would only be here for a semester. While we were sitting in our room one night, Sheila told me she practiced voodoo. I didn't think much about it until one night, when I was looking over my class schedule, I saw Sheila sitting on her bed, focusing on a drinking glass on her desk. She was really concentrating and studying that glass, and suddenly, the glass was floating in mid-air, on its own, for at least twenty seconds. The glass traveled from the desk to her hand. If I hadn't seen it, I would not have believed it. I was living with a witch!

I ran downstairs to the resident director and said, "Please, get me the hell out of that room!"

Unfortunately, there were no more rooms available. From that night on, I slept with one eye open.

Chapter Two

Monday morning, the first day of classes, I was ready. I was a sponge ready to absorb knowledge. Alfred was waiting for me in the lobby. We had breakfast and walked to class together. He saw I was a little nervous and assured me everything would be alright. And he was right: my classes were required freshmen courses, which meant they were easy and boring. All incoming freshmen were tested, and I was placed in the highest level for first year students. I was bored to death, because I knew the course work in my sleep, but they were required courses. I became restless and sought out organizations and clubs to join.

Alfred didn't have much time for me anymore, not like he used to, because it was his senior year and he had a part-time job. My girlfriends were always studying as well.

After dinner one evening, I was sitting on the "Block" (a central location on campus where students went to kick back and relax) reading some poetry, when I saw a group of handsome guys dressed in the colors of black and orange, singing and dancing in a circle. I asked a fellow student sitting next to me, "Who are those guys?"

She replied, "Girl they are only the hottest fraternity on campus."

Indeed, they were hot and cute.

The following day, as I was walking by the Student Union, I noticed a sign that said:

"Wanted: Lady Kittens. All interested please come to the Fraternity House tonight at seven."

Another female student also seemed to be interested in the sign. I had seen her around campus a few times. She asked, "Do you think this meeting is worth attending?"

"Sure, why not?" I said.

"By the way, my name is Jessica Dudley. I am a freshman here at Edgar from Philadelphia."

"Hi, my name is Brenda Peekson. I am also a freshman," I said.

"Yeah, I have seen you on campus. Where are you from, Brenda?"

"You've probably never heard of it, Bloomington, Virginia. It's a small town in the middle of nowhere."

"Yeah, I have heard of that town. I have an aunt who lives there. You're right, it is in the middle of nowhere. Let's go to the meeting tonight," she insisted.

"I'll meet you downstairs in the lobby around 6:30," I suggested.

"Great, see you then."

Jessica and I wore our best outfits to make an impression on the boys in the fraternity. When we arrived at the fraternity house; it was packed. I had never seen so many people in one place in my life.

"Brenda, do you think we have a chance?" Jessica asked.

"We are just as good as anyone in this room."

We signed our names and took a seat. Then the fraternity brothers divided us into small groups to be interviewed.

After every girl had been interviewed, the president of the fraternity said, "The chosen few will be contacted by mail. Thank you all for coming."

On our way back to the dorm, Jessica and I decided to go to the local campus hangout, Melba's Coffee House, for something to eat. It was Friday night and Melba's was jumping. We ordered hamburgers, fries, nachos, and two chocolate shakes. Jessica and I talked, laughed and ate junk food for hours. While we were stuffing our faces, two brothers from the meeting walked in and headed over to our table.

"Hello, ladies, my name is George Alcott, and this is my main man, Brother Jerry Morgan."

Being eager, Jessica invited the boys to join us.

"So, you ladies want to be Lady Kittens. It's a demanding position, you know."

George and Jerry were like two peas in a pod. Great-looking guys with nice personalities and promising futures in their prospective fields. George was a pre-law major, and Jerry majored in economics. We stayed there until Melba began turning the lights out and told us to go home.

That night, Jessica and I began a great friendship. The following week, we went to our mailboxes after class where, to our surprise, we both had letters from the fraternity. They said:

Congratulations, you have been chosen as a "Lady Kitten!"
The first meeting is set for September 25, 1978, at 8:00 p.m.

We were so excited that we jumped up and down, screaming and acting like two crazy fools.

After leaving the post office, I saw Alfred in the hallway. I tried to get his attention, but he rushed off to class and didn't have time to stop. I think he was trying to avoid me for some reason.

At our first meeting as "Lady Kittens," Jessica and I were front row and center. George and Jerry came over to sit with us during the meeting while the other girls looked on, filled with envy. During the course of the meeting, elections were held. I was nominated for president and Jessica for vice president. We both won.

The Lady Kittens were going to have a great year consisting of fundraisers, parties, conferences, seminars, community projects for the youth, and the Annual Fraternity Ball. Jessica and I were in like Flynn, two freshmen girls practically running the campus. I devoted so much of my time to the Lady Kittens, planning events that I did not have much time for anything else, except my classes, which weren't a big deal.

I did manage enough time for dating, however. The new man in my life was George. Jessica was dating Jerry. We always went out together. It was nice, but George and Jerry wanted more. They wanted, and needed, one-on-one attention. They wanted romance, and by this time so did we. George and I had only gone as far as kissing and touching (foreplay) and it was time to take the next step.

After dinner one night, we decided to return to campus, but to Jessica and my surprise, we ended up at an apartment complex.

"George, what are we doing here? I thought we were going back to school."

"Brenda, it's a surprise," he said.

We drove to apartment #147 and got out of the car. George took a key out of his pocket and opened the door.

"Surprise, this is our new place."

Jessica and I knew what this meant: it was time to make love to our men. It was a cute two-bedroom townhouse with French windows, a nice living room, and a spacious kitchen/dining room for me to make romantic dinners for my man. There was wall-to-wall carpeting, as well as one and a half bathrooms. Jerry's room was average with a full-size bed, a dresser, and milk crates stacked on top of each other. They were filled with music albums, and on top of the crates sat a stereo system and a thirteen-inch television set. His bedroom walls were covered with pictures, paddles, and plaques of fraternity paraphernalia.

"Now it's time to see my room, Brenda," George said. "Goodnight, guys."

Jessica looked at me before going into Jerry's room and whispered in my ear, "If you hear any screaming, do not be alarmed. It will only be Jerry. I'm going to take him to another planet."

Jessica was experienced. On the other hand, I was not. George took my hand and led me down the hall to his room. It was the master bedroom and huge, including a king size bed in the middle of the room, bay windows, a walk-in closet, plush ivory carpeting, a nineteen-inch color television, and a stereo system, playing lovemaking music in the background.

"I want you Brenda," he whispered.

Since this was my first time, I didn't know exactly what to do. Sure, I'd read romance novels and magazines; I just hoped they knew what they were talking about.

George held my face and gazed into my eyes as if to hypnotize me. He said, "I know this is your first time, and I promise to be gentle."

I took George at his word and began to relax. He drew me closer to his body, which was warm and hard. His lips brushed against mine and he kissed me. I felt his hot, sweet breath on my neck and my body trembled. His hands caressed my shoulders and slowly moved down my arms and around my waist. He unbuttoned my blouse and kissed my chest as his hands fondled my breasts. I felt my nipples harden with excitement. Then he slowly took my blouse off and unhooked my bra.

I felt free as George explored my round, voluptuous breasts. He carefully unzipped my skirt, and I stood there in my lace panties as George asked me to undress him. I unbuttoned his shirt, button by button, until his chest was exposed. Then I unbuckled his belt as my hands led me to his mountain-like jewel and his pants fell to the floor. I wanted to give myself to him right then and there. He moved me towards the bed where he took off my panties, still kissing and sucking my nipples like a man possessed. George slowly entered me as my hands were gripped to his back. We made passionate love all through the night.

The next morning, I was woken by his kiss. I felt like a new woman. We showered, got dressed, and went downstairs where Jessica and Jerry were having breakfast.

Jessica had a huge grin on her face as she said, "Good morning, guys. Are we hungry? I made bacon, pancakes, scrambled eggs, and coffee. They're all yours."

"Thank you, Jessica," I replied.

After that night, I practically moved into the apartment. I was in love with a great guy. George and I actually dated for a year and a half before I began noticing a change in him. George, who very rarely went home, began spending more time at home all of a sudden. While at his place, I would occasionally answer the telephone, and it would disconnect. Minutes later, the phone would ring again and George would answer it, telling the person to wait a minute as he ran upstairs to take the call in his bedroom. This began happening a lot. I questioned him on it, and he would say:

"It's nothing, Brenda. Don't make this something that it's not."

I was determined to get to the bottom of this. The next time the person called, I would be ready to talk. The following Saturday, I was at the apartment alone, George was at the library, and Jessica had gone out to a movie with Jerry. I was snuggled up on the couch watching television when the phone rang. I said hello and the person hung up. Seconds later, the phone rang again and this time I was pissed. I said, "Who in the hell is this?"

The voice on the other end said, "Veronica. Who in the hell are you?"

"My name is Brenda, George's girlfriend!"

"You may be his girlfriend, but I'm his wife and mother to his soon-to-be son."

I was so upset the phone fell out of my hand and I started crying. I hung up the phone, composed myself, and began packing. After packing, I went downstairs and waited in the dark for George to come home.

Hours later, I heard George open the door and turn on the living room lights. He saw me sitting in the corner with my suitcases.

"Brenda, you startled me. What are you doing sitting in the dark all alone? What's going on?"

"Congratulations, George. Your wife, Veronica, called earlier this evening and wanted to speak with you regarding the baby you two are expecting in a few months."

I didn't give him a chance to come up with any lies or excuses. I picked up my bags and walked out of that place, vowing never to return. I was so angry with George I forgot I didn't have my car. But I refused to go back and ask that jerk for a ride to campus. Luckily, I had enough money to catch the bus. As I was walking to the bus stop, my eyes filled with tears and I felt like such a fool. George was the first man I ever loved, and he used me.

Never again! I told myself.

Chapter Three

As a sophomore, I began concentrating more on my studies and less on men, especially George. I even got a job at a local deli. I actually went home during spring break, just to get away and relax.

One afternoon, I was in the backyard helping my mother pull weeds in her vegetable garden, when an old friend from high school, Justin Scott, drove up with a friend of his.

"Good afternoon, Mrs. Peekson," he said.

"Hello, Justin."

"I heard you were in town. How are you doing, girl?"

"I am doing great. It's good to see you."

"Brenda, I want to introduce you to a friend of mine, Robert Johnson. He is a sophomore at the same school your brother Stephen attends."

"Hello, Robert, it's a pleasure to meet you," I said.

He was a cute guy, in a nerdy kind of way, standing six feet tall with a medium-brown complexion and thick, sandy curly hair. He looked as if he hadn't had much experience with women, which meant he was trainable.

"So, Robert, what's your major?" I asked.

"I'm majoring in mathematics, with a minor in computer science and planning to become a pilot. I want to be one of the next men in space."

"Impressive," I said.

Robert and I exchanged small talk while I continued working in the garden with my mother. Then, out of nowhere, Robert asked me if I would like to have dinner with him. Just as I was trying to forget men existed, here comes another one. I was reluctant, but my mother elbowed me in the ribs and whispered:

"Say yes, girl. He comes from a good family, he's cute, smart, and, besides, he is good looking."

So, I agreed to have dinner.

After Justin's car left the driveway, my mother went on and on. "Brenda, this could be the one, and you should start getting ready for your date; you only have two hours."

"Mother, I am just going on a date; I'm not getting married."

"At any rate, just go in the house and get ready," she insisted.

"Okay, mother dear."

I took a nice, long bubble bath, washed and styled my hair, polished my nails, and slipped on a sundress with a pair of sling back sandals. I went into my mother's room to get her approval.

"Brenda dear, you look lovely. Here is a pair of earrings that would complete the outfit. Also, try some of this French perfume; it smells divine." She smiled.

"Thanks, Mom."

At that moment, the doorbell rang and there stood Robert holding two bunches of pink tulips. "Good evening, Brenda, you look really nice."

"Thank you, Robert, you look dapper yourself. Come in."

"It's nice to see you once again, Mrs. Peekson. I have two bunches of tulips for two beautiful ladies."

"Thank you, Robert. Yes, the flowers are beautiful," I said. "Mother, could you please put the flowers in some water for me?"

"Yes, dear, you two have a good time."

Robert was a sweetheart; he not only opened doors, but pulled out chairs for me as well.

We had a lovely dinner, talking about everything from family, schools, politics, religion, activities, to what we wanted out of life. After dinner, Robert brought me home, opened the door, and kissed me on the cheek. He said he had a nice time and would call me tomorrow.

I had a special feeling about Robert, but I was not about to tell my mother. If she had her way, Robert and I would've gotten married that night. Man of his word: Robert called the next day and invited me out to a picnic in the park. He packed a lunch full of different fruits, salads, chicken and turkey sandwiches, juices, and strawberry shortcake. We found a place under a shaded Magnolia Tree where we laid out the blanket and had a lovely lunch.

Robert and I spent every day with each other until it was time for us to head back to school.

While traveling back, Robert was all I thought about. We would write and call each other every week. For the first time in a long time, I looked forward to going home. I knew Robert really cared about me when he invited me to have dinner with his family. I wanted to meet the people who created such a man.

Weeks later, the day came when it was time to have dinner with the Johnsons. I spent all day getting ready. I wanted everything to be perfect. I wore a simple, yet sophisticated, black sheath dress.

Robert's home was elegant, containing carpeting so plush my feet almost got lost in it, chandeliers hanging from cathedral ceilings, African artwork on the walls, and a wide collection of antique furniture.

Mr. and Mrs. William Johnson III were pillars of the community: he was a neurosurgeon and she, a socialite. Robert also had two sisters named Susan and Robin, who were in boarding school abroad.

I was very nervous when meeting the Johnsons. It was like taking an exam without studying. The Johnson family had a certain aura about them one couldn't help but respect. Mr. Johnson was laid back, with a medium build and height and boy-like qualities; just like Robert. Mrs. Johnson stood tall and was more on the extraverted side; she was outgoing and had a great deal of personality, like myself.

As expected, the questions came fast and furious, mainly from Mrs. Johnson, throughout dinner. I handled her well, however. Even Mr. Johnson and Robert were impressed. I felt Mrs. Johnson was testing me, and I must have passed because we became close. She really wanted to get to know the woman with whom her son was infatuated with.

In my junior year, Jessica and I decided to pledge a sorority, and coincidentally, Robert planned to pledge a fraternity, which meant we would not see each other for at least nine weeks. Being apart from Robert for two months seemed like it would be the longest two months of my life.

As soon as the pledge period was over, we made plans to celebrate together. Robert made reservations at the best hotel in Virginia. We had a lovely suite, including champagne, shrimp cocktail, imported chocolates, and strawberries with whipped cream. Everything was breathtaking.

"Robert, have you done this before?" I asked.

"No, my dad gave me the advice."

While sitting on the oversized bed, we sipped champagne. I picked up the bowl of strawberries, dipping them one-by-one in whipped cream, and fed them to Robert as he fed chocolates to me. I gently kissed him, and suddenly something came over me. The gentle kiss turned into a fiery, passionate kiss. We lost control; it was as if something or someone took control over us. We ripped each other's clothes off like two animals in the heat of passion. Robert covered my body with whipped cream, and I his, as we licked each other's body inch by inch. We enjoyed every part of each other.

Robert entered me passionately in a rhythmic manner, our bodies clapping louder and louder, like an enthusiastic audience at a Soul concert. We reached ecstasy together. That night, we expressed our love to each other.

Morning came, and it was time to check out. I could not wait to call Jessica to tell her I had been to "Paradise."

The next afternoon, as I was packing my car to return to school, Robert called to say he was coming over. He arrived in five minutes flat. We sat on the porch as he gently took my hand.

"Brenda, you are the best thing that has ever happened to me. I love you very much and life has no meaning without you in it." He continued, "After graduation, will you marry me?"

"Oh, yes!" I cried. I was so happy.

I went back to school an engaged woman. As soon as the word got out, all men stayed clear of me, even Alfred. I was a senior and wanted to graduate with honors while planning a country club wedding, which took up most of my time.

One weekend, Robert came home to help plan our wedding, but, for some reason, he didn't seem himself.

"Is everything alright?" I asked.

He held me in his arms and said, "I am so sorry, please forgive me."

"Forgive you for what?"

"We have to postpone the wedding because I am not graduating this year. There's a required course I have to take, which is only offered once a year."

"It's okay; I am a little disappointed, but it's not the end of the world," I told him. "And, besides, we will have the rest of our lives together. We will just postpone the wedding until September 1983. This gives us more time to plan the most beautiful wedding this town has ever seen," I said.

"Brenda, this is why I love you; you are so understanding."

"Oh, Robert."

While driving back to school, I felt tired and worn out, but I thought it was just fatigue. A few weeks later, as Jessica and I were walking across campus, I felt dizzy as if I was going to pass out.

"Are you okay?" she asked. "I'll call 911!"

"No, Jessica, I'm okay, just a little dizzy, that's all."

"Brenda, you haven't been yourself lately. Just promise me you will go see a doctor, and I will go with you."

"I promise. I will make an appointment with a doctor downtown for tomorrow," I said.

The appointment was set for 9:00 a.m. Jess drove me to the doctor's office. I was fine until we entered the waiting room. The medical assistant asked the basic questions and gave me a ton of forms to complete. After completing the forms, I returned to the assistant and she instructed me to have a seat and wait for my name to be called.

"Girl, how are you feeling?" Jessica asked.

"Pretty good, this waiting is taking forever."

Moments later, the nurse entered the waiting room, called my name, and led me into the doctor's office.

"I will be right here for you, Brenda," Jess said.

"Thanks, Jess."

I followed the nurse down the corridor into a room where she took my blood pressure, weight, and temperature. "Ms. Peekson, here is a cup. Can you please go in the ladies' room and produce a urine sample for me?"

After giving the nurse the sample, I went into the patients' room to wait for the doctor.

Moments later, a distinguished woman walked in with a clipboard. "Good morning, Ms. Peekson, I am Dr. Valerie Fuller. How are you this morning?"

"Fine, thank you," I replied.

"Brenda, after looking over your chart and urine sample results, it shows you are pregnant."

"Me! Pregnant with Robert's child! I don't know if I should laugh or cry, doctor. How pregnant am I?"

"You are in your first trimester, about six weeks. I would like to get you started on prenatal vitamins and schedule your next appointment."

"Thank you, doctor."

As I returned to the lobby, I looked at Jessica and she knew. It was like she read my mind. "I will support any decision you and Robert make."

"Thanks, Jess. I have a lot to think about."

I was six weeks pregnant. I knew we weren't ready to become parents, but the thought of having Robert's child was comforting to me. "Jessica, I want to have this baby," I said.

"Well, it seems to me you have already made your decision. But now you have to share the news with Robert."

As soon as I got back to campus, I called Robert and told him I was coming to see him. He met me at the airport; I was too nervous to drive. We went out to dinner and then back to his room. I sat him down, looked him in the eye, and said, "Sweetheart, I love you more than anything and can't wait to be your wife and share the rest of my life with you. But there will be another guest at our wedding."

"Great, who?" he asked.

"Sweetheart, we are going to have a baby," I said.

"A baby! We are going to have a baby? I'm going to be a father? This is great news! Let's share the news with our parents."

"Robert, are you sure this will be good news to them?"

"Of course. They'll be happy for us."

"Whatever you say."

We first drove over to his parents' home to share the news. Robert still had his house key. We entered the living room, where his parents sat listening to jazz music on the stereo.

"Hi, Mom and Dad."

"Mr. and Mrs. Johnson."

"Hi, what's going on? Why are you two here so late?"

"Mom, Dad, what would you say if Brenda and I had a baby?"

"Now, Robert?" his mother asked. "Out of the question. No way." She went on, "No pregnancy before the wedding. Please wait."

"I forbid such a thing!" his father interrupted.

After leaving that house, I was so upset and confused that we didn't even go to see my parents. Robert and I had to make a decision.

"Robert, I want to have this baby."

"I love you, honey, but maybe my parents are right. We can have as many children as we want after we get married."

To our dismay, we decided it would be best to abort our child. That following Monday, I found myself with Robert at an abortion clinic. As we drove up to the clinic, there were pro-life protesters out in front of the building, waving signs and shouting.

"Honey, are you okay with this? We can always come back another time."

"I'm fine," I replied.

Robert protected me and bulldozed through the angry crowd into the clinic. The clinic was set up like a regular doctor's office. I filled out forms, spoke with counselors, and waited. An hour or so later, my name was called. I kissed Robert and went into the sterilized room. The nurse told me to disrobe and lay on the table with my feet in the stirrups until the doctor arrived. The nurse stayed with me as the doctor entered the room. He was a white, middle-aged, balding man with a friendly disposition. All I wanted was to be put to sleep until it was over. I woke up in the recovery room with Robert holding my hand and kissing my forehead, reassuring me everything went well.

I went back to school and for weeks I felt guilty about what Robert and I had done. I believe in pro-choice, but I guess this was the best choice. After a while, things went back to normal. Then it was time for graduation and job interviews. Luckily, I was offered a position as an advertising coordinator at a major agency in North Carolina.

Graduation was a big day filled with joy and sadness. I proved to myself and my family I was truly a strong and independent woman who had made it, but it was only the beginning. Jessica went back home and promised to keep in touch. Robert surprised me with a trip to San Diego to relax before starting my new career.

Chapter Four

I found a nice apartment on the north side of town, which I slowly, but surely, furnished. I arrived at the Martin and Williams Advertising Agency at 8:00 a.m. wearing a navy blue suit and carrying an empty monogramed briefcase. Ms. Jackie Edwards, a perky middle-aged receptionist welcomed and escorted me to the human resources department where I completed a mountain of forms and was informed of the many benefits this company had to offer. Eventually, I was shown to my office. It was nothing special, just four walls, a bookshelf, and a desk with a phone on it. I waited in my office reading the company handbook until my boss arrived. Thirty minutes later, Mrs. Karen Nicolson, the vice president of local accounts, knocked on my door.

"Welcome, Brenda. I hope you had no trouble finding the place with all of the construction going on in town and you are getting settled."

I replied, "Good morning, Mrs. Nicolson. I've had no problem whatsoever and look forward to getting started."

"Just what I want to hear, and please call me Karen. Let me give you a grand tour and introduce you to everyone in the company," she said.

I was introduced to everyone, from the CEO to the mailroom clerk. Then we went back to my office where she gave me a list of my new clients and leads. I caught on quickly and worked my way through the ranks until I became the top biller in the company.

Robert and I saw each other as often as we could. His graduation was coming soon, and he will also be traveling to Germany for special flight training. Robert's parents gave him the biggest graduation/going away party ever, at the country club. There was a band and a sit-down dinner with champagne flowing all through the night.

Then, the day came when it was time for Robert, the love of my life, to go off to Germany. I dreaded that day more than anything. I woke up depressed, but I managed to get myself together and have breakfast with my family. Then the phone rang.

"Hello," I said as I picked up the receiver.

"Good morning, beautiful." It was Robert.

"How are you this morning?" he asked.

"If you want to know the truth, I feel awful about you leaving today. I know you're only going to be gone for a short period of time, and I am acting like a spoiled selfish brat. But the thought of an ocean between us doesn't sit well with me either," I said.

"You aren't acting like a brat. I don't want to go either, but I made a commitment and I want to become a pilot. Once I complete my training in Germany, I'll be on the first flight home to spend the rest of my life with you. My parents are taking me to the airport. Would you like to ride with us?" he asked.

"Of course," I said.

"Great, we will pick you up in fifteen minutes."

"I love you, Robert."

"Right back at you, sweetie."

I hung up the telephone, ran upstairs, and went into my closet to find something special to wear for Robert. I found a Kelly-green cotton scoop neck A-line dress, which was perfect.

The doorbell rang and my mom called out, "Brenda, Robert's here!"

As I stood at the top of the stairs, I saw Robert at the end of the staircase.

He stood there, looking so handsome and distinguished.

"Hello, sweetheart, we have to go now," he said. "Mrs. Peekson, take care of yourself and Brenda while I'm gone."

"I certainly will, and you take care of yourself while in Germany," she replied.

"I will do my best."

As we arrived at the airport, I got a sick feeling that something was going to happen. I kept my feelings to myself for Robert's sake because he was nervous enough. Just then, the ticket agent announced it was time to board the aircraft.

"Well, guys, this is it," Robert said. "Mom, Dad, take care. Thank you both for all you've done for me. I love you both very much. Brenda, I will be counting the days until we are together again. I love you so much. Always remember that."

"I love you too, Robert, and please, please call me once you arrive in Germany."

"I will."

I watched Robert as he walked down the corridor to the airplane. Before he got on the plane, he turned around and blew me a kiss. Holding back the tears, I waved.

Robert called the next day to say he had arrived in Germany safe and sound. We wrote each other every day and called at least once a week. I missed Robert so much I ached. I thought about Robert being away so much I couldn't concentrate on anything else.

Months had passed. I never thought I would get through it, but my baby was coming home in two weeks, and we were going to be married. Everything was set and ready to go for the wedding: the church, my dress, the country club, the band, and our honeymoon to the Greek Islands.

One week before Robert was scheduled to come home, he called. "Hello, almost married woman."

"Hi, almost married man. How are you today, my love?"

"I am doing well. I was just sitting here, thinking about you, and I needed to hear your voice."

"That's so sweet, honey."

"I can't talk long, I just wanted to tell you I love you and will see you soon."

"I love you too, honey, and I can't wait to hold you in my arms again," I replied.

"Bye, baby."

There was something different in Robert's voice when he said, "I love you." I thought maybe he was tired with the time difference.

For some reason, that night I couldn't sleep. Days later, I arrived at work around 9:00 a.m. and there was a message on my desk from Mr. Johnson, Robert's father. Wondering why he would be calling me, I returned his call, but there was no answer. I began to worry and decided to call my mom to see if she had heard anything from the Johnsons.

My mom answered the phone crying, barely able to speak.

"Mom, what's going on?"

"Brenda, honey, I am so sorry!"

"Sorry for what? What's going on?" I demanded.

"Brenda, there has been an accident and Robert is dead."

"What?" I exclaimed.

"Robert was flying during their last training test and, with poor visibility, two planes collided. Robert was in one of the aircrafts that went down, Brenda."

"No, Mom, that can't be! Robert is coming home in two days!"

"I am so sorry, Brenda."

The telephone fell out of my hand and I collapsed in the office. My co-workers found me stretched out on the floor. After coming to, I said, "I have to get home. Someone take me home," I whispered.

"Don't worry about a thing here, take as much time off as you need," my boss said.

"Thank you, Karen."

While driving home to Bloomington, I kept telling myself it couldn't be true. I went straight to Robert's parents' home, hoping this was all a simple mix-up and Robert would greet me at the door. Instead, Mr. Johnson answered the door in tears, which confirmed what I already knew.

"Brenda, our Robert is gone."

"I am so sorry, Mr. Johnson."

"Here we were, planning a wonderful wedding for the two of you, and now we have to plan a funeral."

"I can't believe Robert is gone." I went into the living room, where Mrs. Johnson and the girls were comforting each other.

"I want you to be with us during this time. Robert loved you more than life, and so do we."

The telephone rang and Mr. Johnson answered it. It was Robert's company. The Chief Executive Officer was on the phone to give his condolences and inform us Robert's body had been shipped to the local airport, and he will be transported to the hospital for an autopsy and a positive and legal identification. I didn't want to go to the hospital, but I had to.

It was so silent in the car, you could hear a pin drop; everyone was hoping it was someone else and not Robert. Dr. Ronald White, a coroner, met us at the hospital entrance and took us to the morgue. But before we went in to give a positive identification, Dr. White told us to be prepared if it was Robert. We agreed, holding each other's hands tightly, as we followed Dr. White into the morgue. The morgue was cold and filled with a strong odor of formaldehyde. There, I saw a body frame, covered by a white sheet. As Dr. White went into the room and over to the table, we stood behind a large glass window. We held each other tight, as he pulled the sheet back.

Mrs. Johnson screamed out, "My baby, my baby! God, why did you take my baby?" It was Robert's body lying on the table so still and cold.

After Mr. and Mrs. Johnson positively identified Robert's body, Dr. White escorted us out and gave his condolences.

On the way home, Mr. Johnson stated that arrangements had to be made for a funeral. Days later, when the entire family arrived, we laid Robert to rest.

After losing Robert, I just wanted to die. Life wasn't worth living anymore. Every day was depressing. I woke up, went to work, came home, and went to bed. I was not eating; I wanted to die to be with Robert.

Seeing what was happening to me, my boss strongly recommended I pay a visit to a grief counselor. Somehow, during the course of several months, he convinced me Robert would want me to enjoy life and be happy. I began traveling extensively for my company, meeting a lot of interesting people.

One day, I was walking through the airport struggling with my luggage and a handsome gentleman approached me.

He said, "May I help you with your bags, Miss?"

I was skeptical, but I needed his assistance, so I agreed. As we were walking to my departure gate, he introduced himself as Mr. Anthony Bishop from San Francisco. He was traveling on business to Salt Lake City.

I told him, "My name is Brenda Peekson; I'm traveling on business as well."

Anthony was a well-dressed, well-mannered, Ivy League, GQ type man. "Brenda, would you like to have a drink with me before your flight?" he asked.

"That would be nice, Mr. Bishop. I'll have a tonic water with lime, thank you."

"Call me Anthony or Tony," he said. "What sort of business are you in?"

"I am an advertising executive at a major firm in North Carolina. What about yourself?"

He replied, "I am a real estate developer; I buy and sell commercial properties throughout the country and abroad."

"Anthony, I enjoyed our conversation. Thank you for the drink, and here's my business card. If you are ever in Tar-Hell Country, give me a call."

"I will and here's my card as well."

Around four months later, I was in my office working late on a report on a Friday evening. Jackie, the receptionist, called to say there was someone here to see me. I asked her who and she said she was given instruction not to announce him. Annoyed, I went to the lobby and there stood Mr. Ivy League with a dozen beautiful yellow roses.

"Anthony, what are you doing here?" I asked.

"I am here on business and pleasure, and these flowers are for you," he said.

"Thank you, they are gorgeous."

"You are more than welcome. The flowers are just like you, Brenda," he said with a grin. "Why don't you call it a night, as far as work, so we can go out on the town?"

"Where would you like to go?" I asked.

"Leave it to me; I will take care of everything."

"Considering you are not from the area, you sure know a lot about my city," I said.

"I like to get to know the cities I visit," he replied.

"So, where are we going?"

"First, I am going to take you to the best five-star restaurant in the city."

I had lived here for seven years and never knew about this place. It was an elegant restaurant with valet parking, a four string quartet, chandeliers, white linen everywhere, and a first-rate wait staff. We walked in and the maître d' showed us to our table. Anthony took the liberty of ordering our wine and dinner. Most men loved doing that stuff; it made them feel in control, so I let him. Anthony was an adventurous person and loved to try new things. He wanted me to try new things as well.

The waiter came with our appetizers.

"Anthony, what are these?" I asked.

"Escargot, sweetheart," he said.

"Snails! You honestly expect me to eat this? I had no idea you were ordering snails," I continued.

"Come on, Brenda, try them. If you don't like them, then don't eat them, but at least give the snails a chance."

"Well, I have grown up eating pork intestines, so I guess a few snails couldn't be all bad."

"Good, go ahead. Eat one."

"Okay."

"What do you think?" he asked as I put it in my mouth.

"Not bad, not bad at all, actually," I said, surprised.

"See, always try something new at least once."

Anthony was right; the dinner and conversation were excellent. After dinner, he suggested we go dancing, which was a good idea since I hadn't gone out since Robert's death. We went to an upscale dance club on the east side of town. As we entered the club, people from everywhere came up to greet Anthony as if we were celebrities or something. It was a sophisticated club—members only, very classy. Anthony's friends bought us drinks, as well as food, all through the evening. And we danced the night away. The next thing I knew it was 3:30 a.m., and I was still going. I had an energy I never knew existed in me.

"Brenda, it's getting late. Would you like to go home now?"

"No, not really. Believe it or not, I'm not tired."

"Great, let's go out for an early breakfast."

"Will they serve breakfast this early, or do you know the chef at the restaurant as well?"

"As a matter of fact, I do," he said.

"It figures," I sighed.

After a light breakfast, Anthony drove me home, walked me to my door, kissed me on the cheek, and said he'd had a great time. I thought it was weird, in a nice way that he didn't ask to come in for coffee, since I knew what "coffee" meant. I found myself dreaming about Anthony that night. I fantasized about what he would be like in bed.

The next morning, I dropped Anthony a thank you card in the mail, but I didn't hear a word from him. I decided he was just playing games. But life went on, and so did I.

One afternoon, I was coming back to my office from a client meeting, when the phone rang.

"Brenda, girlfriend, how in the hell are you?"

"Jessica?" I inquired

"Yes, it's me, girl. What's up?" she asked.

"Oh, nothing. I'm just working and trying to make it like everyone else, girl."

"The reason I'm calling is to ask if you'd like to go on a seven-day cruise with me to St. Thomas in a few weeks. My treat. A little sun, fun, girl talk, and man watching. What do you say?"

"It sounds like fun, but I'm too busy to leave now," I said.

"Stop it. You are just making excuses. You haven't really gone anywhere since Robert's accident. Do you honestly think Robert would want you to live like a hermit?" she asked.

"No," I sighed.

"Well, change your schedule, and I will meet you in Miami, Florida."

She booked us on a singles cruise. I love her. I arrived at the ship and checked in first.

Later, Jessica arrived with five pieces of luggage in hand.

"Hey, girl, it's so good to see you!" she yelled.

"You look great; you are still thin, beautiful, and crazy!" I yelled back.

"Thanks, girl. You look amazing as well. Brenda, rule number one is always be ready."

"You certainly are," I said jokingly.

"Let's unpack, change into our bathing suits, and hit the pool."

"How's Jerry these days?"

"Who? Girl, Jerry and I are history."

"I'm sorry, what happened?"

"I caught him cheating on me with some bimbo from his office. I hate to say it, but birds of a feather stick together."

"Are you still with the same accounting firm?" I asked.

"Yes, and I am now a certified public accountant."

"Awesome, I am so happy for you. You were always a whiz with numbers."

"George is the proud father of a little boy, George Jr., but he and his wife are on the verge of killing each other. And every time I see him, he asks about you. He still loves you and wants you back. There have been times when he wanted to pick up the phone and call you, but he was afraid of being rejected."

"That ship has sailed, and enough about George and Jerry. What's new with you, Jess?"

"Nothing much, girl; the same day-to-day crap."

"Is there anyone special in your life?" I asked.

"Sure, I am dating, but there's no one special in my life. I find men don't know what they want. For example, men say they want an intelligent, secure, independent, and professional lady who is her own woman. They want someone who is a proper lady in public and a whore in bed. You know, women like us. Once they find a woman like that, they don't know what to do with her. I find men are intimidated by us. Men aren't in control like they used to be, and they can't deal with it," she went on.

"Sure, there are men out there who are scum, but there are also good, single men out there who are secure with themselves and welcome women like you and me."

"Wake up, Cinderella, you may find the so-called *good men*, but most of us end up with jerks."

"Not true; I have had my share of jerks as well."

Jessica and I had a wonderful cruise. We didn't find any good men, but it was great to see my best friend. I returned to work relaxed and ready to tackle the world. I was full of energy and zest.

One evening, I was home cooking dinner when there was a knock at the door. I opened it and no one was there, only a dozen of yellow roses with a card that said:

"To Brenda:
Love always,
Anthony B."

Anthony was in town.

I wondered what was up his sleeve. He was so mysterious, in a sexy, James Bond kind of way. He definitely kept me intrigued. I felt like a horse with a big, juicy carrot dangling in front of me. Even though we hadn't been intimate, yet, I wanted that carrot.

I put the roses in a vase in my bedroom so they would be the last thing I saw at night, as well as the first thing in the morning. I woke up moist between my legs the next morning after dreaming about Anthony and me doing the "Wild Thing."

Realizing it was only a dream, I got up and dressed for work. It was a beautiful spring day: the sun was shining, birds were singing, and there was also the sound of children playing. As I headed out the door, Anthony came up the driveway wearing a tailor-made tan suit and a smile. My legs tingled all over again.

Anthony gently kissed me on the cheek. "Brenda, may I come in?" he asked politely.

"I'm sorry, yes. Please, come in. Thank you for the flowers. They were beautiful."

"You are welcome."

"Anthony, it is good to see you, but what are you doing here on a Friday morning?"

"I'm here to take you away for the weekend to Key West, Florida. The plane leaves in three hours."

"Are you crazy?" I asked.

"No, just adventurous."

"I would love to go, but there's a little matter called work, remember?"

"Why don't you call in sick? Today is Friday. I am sure it's slow at the office, and besides, I want to spend the weekend with you in sunny Key West."

It was difficult to say no to Anthony about anything. He had that way about himself. The next thing I knew, I was on the telephone with my office.

"Good morning, Martin and Williams Advertising, may I help you?"

"Good morning, Jackie," I said.

"Brenda, is that you?" she asked.

"Yes, Jackie."

"You sound awful."

"I don't feel well, and will not be in today."

"Stay home to rest and drink lots of hot tea," she insisted.

"I will, thanks, and I will see you on Monday," I said.

"Brenda, you deserve an Oscar for that performance. Now, pack a few things and let's head to the airport," Anthony said.

"Key West is so beautiful. This is heaven on earth with palm trees, swaying in the breeze and sandy white beaches with miles and miles of blue ocean waters. This is one of my favorite places. Let's check in."

We stayed at an exclusive hotel on the beach with a spacious balcony. Everyone in the hotel, once again, treated Anthony as if he were royalty. They seemed to know him personally.

"How do they know you so well?" I asked.

"Whenever I am in Key West, I stay at this hotel," he said.

We checked into our room, unpacked, and hit the streets for some sightseeing. We went shopping, had some lunch, and returned to the hotel to change into our bathing suits to go to the beach for some sun for the rest of the afternoon.

When we returned, Anthony said, "Brenda, honey, go back to the room and get dressed for dinner."

"What exotic place do you have in mind this time?" I asked.

"Let me surprise you."

We showered, changed, and jumped in a taxi.

"Where to, sir?" the taxi driver asked.

"The Pier Three Hundred Restaurant please," Anthony said.

The Pier Three Hundred, was near the hotel on the beach. It was a five-star restaurant, overlooking the cobalt blue Atlantic Ocean. Anthony and I stuffed ourselves with oysters, clams, and shrimp scampi, as well as a few bottles of wine.

"Brenda, after dinner, would you like to take a walk along the beach and stop by this amazing jazz club in the area?"

"I'm a little tired. I'd like to go back to the hotel, if that's alright with you?" To be honest, my mind was on that king size plush bed in the room. Finally after we made it through dinner and dessert, we went back to the hotel.

"I'm going to jump in the shower. I'll be out in ten minutes or so."

"That's fine, sweetie."

It was time to make my move. I lit scented candles throughout the room. I dimmed the lights and put on some romantic music. Then, I opened a bottle of chilled wine and headed for the bathroom in the nude. I slid the shower door open ever so gently, so as not to disturb Anthony. His back was facing me as I slipped my hands around his waist. He jumped with excitement and he turned around smiling. I lathered my hands and caressed his monstrous-like chest, feeling my nipples harden. We covered our bodies with lather as I felt Anthony's member stiffen against my thigh. My hand followed every curve of his body like a car on the highway to heaven. We held each other tightly, not wanting to let go. My body tingled all over. I wanted so much for Anthony to make love to me.

We rinsed our bodies off and Anthony gave me a long, hot, and passionate kiss as he carried me to bed and we made passionate love until dawn.

"Good morning, sunshine," he said the next morning.

"Good morning, Anthony. Thank you for an unforgettable evening."

"No, thank you, honey. I took the liberty to order breakfast for us."

"Great, because I am starving!" I said.

"What would you like to do after breakfast?" he asked.

"Make love to you," I replied.

"That sounds good."

"What would you like to do after lunch and dinner?" I asked.

"Make more sweet love to you." He smiled.

I didn't want the weekend to end, but it did. As we were on our way back to our destinations, Anthony grabbed me, gave me a long kiss, and pulled out a two-carat diamond ring from his pocket.

He said, "Brenda, I love you. Will you marry me?"

Still high from the weekend, I exclaimed, "Yes, Anthony! I will marry you!"

I rushed home to tell my family and friends, thinking they would be happy for me, but they were not. My mother told me not to marry Anthony, given the fact I hardly knew him.

"You have never met his parents or his friends. For all you know, Anthony could be a murderer!" she said.

"Mom, Robert is gone. I am moving on with my life, and so should you. I am an adult; I make my own decisions. You cannot tell me what to do. Besides, I'm in love with Anthony Bishop!"

Everything was happening so fast. The wedding was to be held in six months, and I had not even started planning. Anthony relocated to North Carolina where we bought a lovely home in the suburbs. We had a picture-perfect wedding. Even though my family wasn't thrilled about the idea, they made a good show. Everyone attended the wedding, except Anthony's parents, who were called out of the country suddenly.

After the honeymoon, things began to change. Anthony became very insecure. He would call me five times a day and come to my office unannounced. He was clearly not the man I thought I married. He turned into a hen-pecked puppy. He would do anything I asked him to do, even jump into the lake. He worshiped me; I could do no wrong. Even when I was clearly wrong, to him I was right. I lost all respect for him because he had no backbone. The man never stood up for himself.

Jessica didn't understand. "Brenda, are you crazy? Good men are hard to find, don't you realize that?" she said. "If you don't want him, trust me, there are thousands of women out there who would be more than happy to take him off your hands, my friend," she pleaded.

"They may get that chance," I replied.

"It's only been a few months. Give your marriage a chance," she said.

I began to stay out more, taking more business trips and really getting involved in community organizations. I would do anything not to go home to Anthony. Finally, I realized this so-called marriage was not going anywhere and decided to do something about it.

After dinner one night, I sat Anthony down and explained to him we had a problem with our marriage. In order to save the relationship, we had to seek counseling. Anthony didn't feel as if there was a problem and didn't want to see a counselor.

At this point, I had no choice but to file for divorce. Anthony did not fight me. He was very fair; he just wanted me to be happy. We split everything fifty/fifty and went our separate ways. To my surprise, no one said, "I told you so," —not to my face, anyway.

After the divorce, I became busier than ever and was given an entire new list of clients, which was great for getting my mind off of my own troubles. There was one major client, Mr. Morgan Walsh, Jr., whose family owned a chain of food stores across the country.

I was going to have my first meeting with him.

When I was sitting in my office, getting ready for the meeting, Jackie came in. "Brenda, Mr. Walsh is here to see you," she said.

"Good, please show him in. Good afternoon, Mr. Walsh."

"Good afternoon, Mrs. Peekson."

"It's *Ms.*" I corrected him.

"Sorry."

"That's okay."

"Why don't we have a seat and get started?" I suggested.

"Good idea, Ms. Peekson."

"Mr. Walsh, we here at Martin and Williamson have come up with some "can't lose" ideas that will promise to take Walsh Groceries through the roof in profits this year with heavy print and media, including billboard advertising with considerable amounts of commercials on both the local and national level. Mr. Walsh, right now we want to target women between the ages of twenty and sixty-five. Let's face it, women still do the majority of the grocery shopping and watch more television than men."

"Ms. Peekson, you have really done your homework. I am impressed," he said.

"Thank you, sir."

"Please, call me Morgan, since it looks like we will be doing business together."

"Do you mean it, Morgan?" I asked.

"I just have to go back to the office and talk it over with my dad, Morgan Walsh, Sr. but I do not see any problem whatsoever. I will give you a call to-morrow."

"Well, in that case, welcome to Martin and Williamson. You won't be sorry," I said.

"I know."

As soon as Morgan left, my boss came into my office. "Brenda, congratula-tions, you have done it once again. This is a major account. The entire office is buzzing over this one. I want you to devote all your time to this account."

"What about my other accounts?"

"Don't worry about them. I'll handle it."

"You are the boss," I replied.

I always looked forward to seeing Morgan, especially when I was having a bad day because he would always make me smile. The more we saw each other, the closer we became as friends. We even went out once or twice together, which was not a good idea mixing business with pleasure. One day while going over the campaign with Morgan, he stopped what he was doing and took my hand.

"I really like and enjoy your company and would like to spend more time with you," he said.

"I enjoy your company as well, and would like to get to know you better. But, I would not feel comfortable dating you while we are working on this project," I replied. As soon as the Morgan Groceries Campaign is completed, I would love to see you out of the office."

"I respect your decision, and I might add you are one classy and professional lady."

"Thank you, you're a class act yourself."

Six months later, the Walsh Campaign was completed and everyone was happy. Mr. Morgan Walsh, Sr. was so pleased with everything he gave a huge party on his yacht honoring my company, Martin and Williamson, for doing a great job. Everyone at the party looked like royalty. The ladies wore designer ballroom gowns and the men wore dashing tuxedos.

"Good evening, Brenda. You look sensational this evening."

"Thank you, you look very handsome."

"Well, thank you."

"Everything looks so nice. This is a beautiful yacht, Morgan."

"Yes, my dad knows how to live. The campaign is over; can we date now?"

"Yes, I don't see why not," I answered.

"Good, consider this our first date," he said.

"Let me introduce you to my family."

"Mother, may I introduce you to the woman who put Walsh Groceries on the map, Ms. Brenda Peekson."

"Good evening, Mrs. Walsh, it is such a pleasure to finally meet you in person. Morgan speaks very highly of you."

"Well, thank you, Brenda, the pleasure is all mine."

"And you know my dad, Mr. Morgan Walsh, Sr.," Morgan gestured.

"It's good to see you again. Thank you so much for making this all possible," he said.

"You are more than welcome, but it was a team effort," I told him.

"Now that we have made the rounds, let's leave. I know a nice place where it's quiet."

"It sounds nice, but wouldn't it be rude to leave now?"

"No, it wouldn't. Wait here and I'll get our coats."

"Let's say our goodbyes first. Where are we going?"

"Over to my house. You've seen how my dad lives, now I want you to see how I live."

Morgan's home was immaculate. He had the finest Italian Corinthian leather furniture, wonderful paintings, and works of art, fine china, and crystal. The house was so clean with everything in place, one would think a woman lived there.

"Come on in and relax. What can I get you?"

"A glass of Pinot Grigio, please."

"Here we go, two glasses of Pinot," he said, extending a glass in my direction.

"Thank you, Morgan. You have beautiful home, such exquisite taste."

"I decorated myself. Let me give you a tour."

"Lovely."

"We are in the living room. Right here is the chef's kitchen, but there's no chef, and here we have the dining room, as well as a greenhouse for my plants, and upstairs we have the bedrooms, fully equipped with bathrooms fit for a king and queen."

"Why do you have so many bedrooms?" I asked.

"I have a lot of friends who think my home is a hotel. That's one of the reasons I bought it. And this is the master bedroom; do you like it?"

"This is beautiful. It's so huge, a family of four could live in this room alone."

"You are so funny, Brenda. I really like you and want to see you as much as I can. Are you seeing anyone, seriously?"

"No."

"I want us to be an item and go places and do things together," he said.

"I want the same."

"May I kiss you?" he asked.

"And a gentleman to boot. Yes, you may kiss me." Afterwards, I said, "It's getting late. Can you take me home now?"

"Are you feeling alright?" he asked.

"I will take you home. Get some rest and I'll call you tomorrow." And the next day he called. "Hello sweetheart, how are you this morning?" he asked.

"I am much better thank you."

"Brenda, my dad and I just had a meeting, and with all the success from the campaign, he is opening stores in Arizona. He wants me to go there to set things up."

"How long will you be gone?"

"I'm leaving this afternoon and should be gone for a couple of weeks. When I return, we will do all the things I promised."

Morgan fell in love with Arizona's weather, as well as its people. He stayed in Arizona longer than necessary because he loved it so much. Morgan called from Tucson: "Hello, love. I am coming home this evening and want to stop by your place to see you."

"Hi, Morgan, long time no hear. What time should I expect you?"

"My plane arrives at five. So, I figure around six-ish this evening."

"I will see you then." I had only a few hours to clean the place and look decent. I managed to clean the house and slip on a skirt and blouse before Morgan arrived.

"Hi, sweetie," he said. "Come here and kiss your man."

"Come in. How was Arizona?"

"It's one of the most beautiful states in the country. It's so beautiful I would love to move there."

"Are you serious?"

"Yes, I'm serious."

"Have you spoken with your dad about this?"

"Not yet. I plan to tell him this evening. How have you been? I've missed you so much, Brenda."

"I have been busy with work. I am working on a new account."

"You must be stressed out," he said.

"A little."

"Can I relieve some of that stress for you?"

"Only as you can, Morgan." Suddenly, the phone rang. "This better be good," I said. "Hello?"

"Hello, Ms. Peekson, how are you?" It was Morgan's father.

"Just fine, Mr. Walsh," I said.

"By any chance have you heard from Morgan?" he asked.

"As a matter of fact, he's right here, just a moment."

"Hello, Dad, I'll be right there. Brenda, as you heard, I have to go. I'll call you later."

"Give me a kiss," I said.

"Bye, babe."

After Morgan saw his father that evening, he changed his mind about relocating to Arizona. I am sure his father had a lot to do with his decision. Even though Morgan was an adult, his father still called the shots.

I hadn't heard from Morgan since he told me he was not going to Arizona, so I decided to call him, but a woman answered the telephone.

"Hello, may I speak with Morgan?" I asked.

"I'm sorry, he isn't here at the moment. Would you like to leave a message?"

"Yes, can you please have him call Brenda?"

"I certainly shall."

"Thank you."

I wondered why there was a woman answering Morgan's home telephone. I did not question him on it because the woman on the telephone didn't give me a reason. I trusted Morgan. We even opened an IRA and a Money Market Account together.

A few days later, I called Morgan to ask him out to dinner, and the same woman answered the telephone. She was polite, but now it was time for me to ask some questions.

"Morgan, are you entertaining any guest at your home?" I asked.

"No, why?"

"There is a woman who answers your telephone when you aren't at home. Who is it?"

"Oh, that's my sister Samantha who goes by the name Sam. She's from Seattle."

"I didn't know you had a sister," I said.

"Yes, she is the daughter no one talks about."

"Why?"

"She's different."

"What do you mean, she's different?"

"She's bi-sexual and everyone, except me, in the family disowned her. So, when she comes to town, she stays at my place."

"That's too bad."

"Brenda, I have no secrets from you."

Morgan was very sincere, but I wanted to verify his story with other family members. However, I was not close enough to them to speak on the subject. Morgan sensed I was uneasy about his story, so he suggested we all go out to dinner.

"That would be nice. I want to meet as much of your family as possible," I said.

"Tomorrow night, dinner at the Japer Room, the three of us."

"Sounds good, I will meet you and Sam there at seven."

I arrived early and got a table.

"Hello, honey," he said.

"Hi, sweetheart, and this must be Sam, I replied. It is a pleasure to meet you. I am Brenda, the woman who is always calling and bugging you about Morgan's whereabouts."

"Excuse me?" she asked.

"Why don't we all have a seat?" he gestured.

"What does everyone have a taste for tonight?"

"Before we order, Morgan, I would like to get to know Sam a little bit better," I said.

"Brenda, I forgot to tell you, Sam has to leave right after dinner. She has plans with a friend tonight."

"Oh, really? Well, let's order," I insisted.

Morgan rushed through dinner, paid the check, and we were out the door. The evening felt really strange. Morgan dropped Sam off at his place, and he and I went to my place. We went into the living room and sat down. Morgan was in a strange mood.

"Sweetheart, are you alright?" I asked consoling.

"Yes, I'm fine. I just want to hold you," he said.

"I can do that."

"Brenda, will you marry me?"

"Excuse me? Morgan, can I think about this?" I asked nicely. I was not keen on the idea, considering my track record, and besides, I did not love him enough to marry him. You would think I said yes because Morgan began taking me to reception halls, churches, bridal shops, caterers, photographers, bands, and even to meet with clergy. We were looking at wedding stuff so much I almost forgot to make a doctor's appointment. Luckily, I didn't.

I went to the doctor, and to my surprise, I was pregnant again, this time with Morgan's child.

That night at dinner, I told Morgan I was pregnant. He seemed happy, but was not convinced until we both went to the doctor for an ultrasound. From then on, I knew this relationship was all downhill. I humored him and we went to the doctor for the ultrasound. I laid on the table and the doctor covered my stomach with a gel. Morgan was right there, front and center, watching the screen.

"Ms. Peekson, everything is fine. The baby is doing well. I can even tell you the sex, if you wish," the doctor said.

"Yes, I would like to know."

"You are having a little girl."

"Brenda, I am so happy, we are having a little girl," Morgan said.

I told my parents I was pregnant and they were happy for me, but wished I was married.

For the first few months, Morgan was very attentive and loving. He would get and do anything I asked. He rubbed my back, feet, made dinner, or whatever I needed. During the first trimester, Morgan was there for me. Then during my fourth month, things changed for the worst. He stopped coming by to visit or even call. I called Morgan at work, but he was never there, and he wouldn't return my calls. When I called him at home, I either got his answering machine or his sister, who was polite as usual, but there was something different in her voice; the woman who was answering Morgan's home telephone was soft and passive.

What in the hell is going on here? I asked myself. *Let me call Jessica; she will know what to do*, I thought.

"Jessica?"

"What's wrong? Why are you crying?" she asked.

"My life is screwed up. I am so confused."

"Calm down, take a deep breath."

"I am seven months pregnant and I haven't seen or heard from Morgan in three months. Every time I call him, he's never in the office and doesn't return my calls. I am carrying his child. And to top it all off, when I call him at home, a woman answers the telephone, and it doesn't sound like his sister. Jessica, have I lost him?"

"What does the woman sound like?"

"She is nice and very polite to me when I call."

"That's strange, because if a woman calls a man's home more than once, and I answer the telephone, I'm going to ask her some questions, like who in the hell are you, and what do you want with my man?"

"I agree."

"To put your mind at ease, you should get in your car and go over there to see what's going on. But you shouldn't go alone in your condition."

"The only person I would want to go with me is you, and that's not possible. I will go alone. I don't want everyone to know that I am a fool."

"Be optimistic; there could be a simple explanation for all of this."

"Sure, well, I'm going over there right now, and I'll call you later." I hung up with Jess, got in my car, and drove to Morgan's home.

I took a deep breath, walked up to Morgan's door, and rang the doorbell. A woman answered the door and it wasn't Samantha.

"Hello, may I help you?" she asked.

"Hi, is Morgan here?" I asked, almost in tears.

"No, but he is due back shortly. Are you alright?" she asked "Come in. Let me get you something to drink."

"Thank you."

"Is there anything I could do until Morgan arrives?"

"Yes, who are you?" I asked.

"I'm sorry, my name is Sarah Brooks, Morgan's girlfriend."

That's when I really broke down and cried.

"You shouldn't get so upset, especially in your condition."

"Sarah, my name is Brenda Peekson. Morgan and I have been dating for three years, and I am carrying his baby."

"You liar! I don't believe you! Morgan would never do such a thing to me! What do you want, money?"

"No, I don't want money; I want the truth! How do you think I feel? I am pregnant with his child. He asked me to marry him, and we were looking at churches, reception halls, bridal dresses, and homes."

"What?"

"I called him many times when you answered the telephone."

"Many times," she said. "Brenda, I have only been back in North Carolina for a couple of months so it was not me."

"Morgan told me that was his sister Samantha and she was gay."

"Morgan is an only child."

"No!" I shouted.

"Morgan and Sam are great friends, and yes, she is gay."

"You said you just came back to North Carolina. Where were you?"

"My company sent me to Arizona for a while. Morgan and I were planning to move there, but he suddenly changed his mind."

"Oh my God, Morgan told me his father sent him to Arizona to oversee the opening of new stores in that area."

"That son of a bitch!" she shouted. "Brenda, didn't you think something was strange when he would not bring you here?"

"I came here all the time. I know where everything is in this house. We even had our first Thanksgiving dinner here together in his home."

"Correction, *my* home."

"You mean this is not Morgan's house?"

"No, it's not. Morgan lives with me. The deed is in my name."

"How can that be? Morgan can afford anything he wants."

"Another correction; Morgan's father can afford anything he wants, not the son.

Morgan Sr. has Morgan Jr. on a monthly allowance. Brenda, when you came over to my home did you not see signs of a woman living here?"

"Of course, I did, and when I questioned it, he just said they belonged to Sam, his sister. Sarah, I had no reason not to trust him. Morgan and I would go out with his friends Larry, Susan, Mike, Jasmine, Harvey, and Charmaine."

"They aren't just Morgan's friends, they are/were my friends as well. Brenda, my so-called friends, never mentioned a word about you."

"Sarah, your name never came up either."

"That asshole!" she said.

"I don't know about you, but I am finished with Morgan!"

"What about the baby?" she asked.

"I will make a way for me and my child."

"No, I will step aside. A child needs both parents."

"I could never trust Morgan again, and besides, there are a lot of single mothers out here who are doing just fine."

"Brenda, I don't know who I feel sorrier for, you or me."

At that moment, the door opened and Morgan walked in. "Hello Sarah, baby I'm home."

"Hi, I am in the living room. We have company."

"Oh, yeah, who is it?"

"It's the mother of your soon-to-be child."

"Hello, Morgan," I said.

"Oh shit!" he sighed. "What are you doing here, Brenda?"

"Getting at the truth, something you are not familiar with!"

"Morgan, how could you lie and cheat on Brenda and me, two women who love you so much and would do anything for you?"

"I am carrying your child, Morgan. Does that mean anything to you?"

"Say something, dammit!"

"I am so sorry."

"Sorry, is that all you can say? You have devastated three lives here!"

"I hate you and don't ever want to see you again! Sarah, will you please help me out of this chair so I can get the hell out of here?"

"I will help you," Morgan gestured.

"Don't touch me! The sight of you makes me sick!" I said.

43

"Brenda, I am so sorry," Sarah said.

"So am I, Sarah. So am I."

Driving home, I felt sick. I had been used once again by a man who claimed he loved me. I opened the front door to my telephone ringing. It was Jessica.

"Girl, I have been trying to reach you for hours. What happened?"

"What do you think happened? Morgan is a liar and cheater. I was right; he is involved with another woman, and she owns the house they live in!"

"Was Morgan there?" she asked.

"Not at first, he came later."

"What did he have to say for himself?"

"All he said was he was sorry."

"What could he say? He got caught. I am so sorry, Brenda."

"Me too."

• • • • •

I was doing a light workout at home, when my water suddenly broke and I went into labor. I didn't want to call Morgan, but I had no choice. Morgan was my baby's father.

"Hello, Sarah, is Morgan there?" I asked.

"Yes, just a moment," she said.

"Morgan, my water just broke. Can you come to my house as soon as possible and take me to the hospital?"

"I'm on my way!" Morgan arrived to my home in five minutes flat. "Come on, sweetheart, the car is running. I have your suitcase."

We arrived at the hospital just in time. I was wheeled into labor and delivery by the nurse as Morgan stayed by my side.

The doctor came in and said, "Okay, Brenda, this is it. You have dilated ten centimeters. I want you to push when I tell you."

"Okay, doctor," I said.

"Here we go, push."

"You're doing great."

"Morgan, where are you?" I asked.

"I'm right here, sweetheart," he replied.

"Brenda, I see his head. We are almost there. Push. You're doing great, Brenda. One more big push should do it," said the doctor. "Here we go."

"I can't push anymore!"

"You can do this, Brenda!" Morgan said.

"No, I can't. Let this baby stay in me! It hurts too much!"

"Brenda, you are about to give life to our child, our angel, someone we will share the rest of our lives with. You can do this!"

"This is the last push," the doctor said. "Give me a big one! Here she comes. Brenda, she is beautiful. Keep pushing; don't stop until I tell you to."

"Is she out yet?" I asked.

"Almost. Stop, she has arrived. Brenda, you did great!"

"Thank you, doctor."

"She is so beautiful. She looks just like you with her beautiful pecan tanned complexion and curly hair."

Once again, Morgan was attentive and caring. He came over to the house every-day bearing food and gifts for our new born daughter, Breanna Nicole Walsh. We were like a little family. Knowing it was not going to last, I took advantage of every moment by taking much needed naps, errands, doing chores, and catching up with some work from the office. I must admit, I did enjoy the time we spent together.

My maternity leave went by quickly, and it was time for me to return to work.

"Brenda, I don't want you to go back to work," Morgan told me. "A child should be at home with her mother for the first year, instead of in some daycare."

"That's all well and good for some mothers, but I have to go back to work. I just hoped you would support my decision."

"Okay, I will support your decision. What else can I do?"

"I'll take care of Breanna's needs as far as diapers, formula, toys, cribs, playpens, food, clothes, etc. What I'd like for you to do is to take care of the babysitter's weekly payment."

"I don't know anything about this so-called babysitter who's going to be with my child."

"Our child."

"Fine, our child."

"Her name is Mrs. Sally Bowman. She lives right across the street. She is a sixty-five-year-old retired first grade teacher and grandmother of five. She and Breanna get along very well; she is good with her."

"How much does she charge per week?"

"Only one hundred dollars per week," I said.

"I will take care of the babysitter's payment, but I still want to meet her first," he said finally.

"I have no problem with that."

Things were going fine the first few weeks or so. The first week after returning to work, Morgan picked Breanna up from the babysitter and paid Mrs. Bowman. The second week was like pulling teeth to get Morgan to pay Mrs. Bowman. By the third week, I was at my wit's end.

"Morgan, Mrs. Bowman wants her money for taking care of Breanna," I said.

"You got paid this week. Why don't you pay the woman?" he said.

"That was not our agreement."

"Okay, I will pay the dam woman!"

"What's wrong with you?" I asked.

"I don't want to be a part of this anymore."

"Morgan, you promised!"

"I did not promise anything to you. I'm leaving."

"If you walk out on me and Breanna, trust me, you will live to regret it!"

"Goodbye, Brenda."

I gave Morgan every opportunity to take care of his responsibilities. I wrote and called him, but he never returned my calls. He acted as if Breanna and I did not exist anymore. Thus, I hired Attorney Lauren Canty, to help me obtain child support.

"Ms. Peekson, it's nice to meet you, and thank you for coming," she said. "My office and I have unsuccessfully tried to get in contact with Mr. Morgan Walsh. But he did leave a voice message with my assistant stating he will not pay any child support. I have subpoenaed Mr. Walsh's financial records."

"Ms. Canty, I don't understand it. Morgan's family is worth a great deal of money, but he doesn't want to help support his child."

"Ms. Peekson, this is not uncommon. It is usually the ones who have the funds who cause the most problems. It's more of a control issue than anything else. I have scheduled a court date for next Wednesday at 9:00 a.m. You and Morgan are expected to be there. Mr. Walsh has responsibilities in which he has failed to meet."

"Does he know this?" I asked.

"Yes, a constable was sent over to his office yesterday. I will see you at the courthouse next week."

I went home after meeting with Ms. Canty feeling confident she would come through for Breanna and me.

Wednesday morning at 9:00 a.m. sharp, I was in Family Court with my attorney and the judge.

"Good morning, Ms. Canty," I said.

"Good morning, Ms. Peekson. How are you feeling today?"

"A bit nervous," I replied.

"That's normal. I don't see Mr. Walsh or his attorney."

"Neither do I," I said. "What happens if he doesn't show?"

"It will help us and hurt his case."

"All rise, court is now in session. The Honorable Judge Mark Waterson presiding," the bailiff said.

"Please be seated. Case number 754302, Peekson vs. Walsh. Are all parties here?" the judge asked.

"No, your Honor, Attorney Canty and my client, Brenda Peekson, are present."

"We have waited long enough. If Mr. Walsh, was planning to be here, he would have been here by now. Continue, Attorney Canty."

"Thank you, your Honor. My client is suing for sole custody and child support for her daughter, Breanna Nicole Walsh. The father, Morgan Walsh, refuses to help support the child in any way. Mr. Walsh is financially stable to support Breanna with no problem, whatsoever, your Honor."

"The fact he did not bother to show up this morning says a lot about this man," the judge concluded. "I rule in favor of the plaintiff, Ms. Brenda Peekson."

"Ms. Peekson will have sole custody, and Mr. Walsh is ordered to pay child support of $900.00 a week, now until the child turns eighteen years old. Court is adjourned."

"Thank you so much, Ms. Canty," I said.

"It was a pleasure. Once the child support payments are garnished from Mr. Walsh's payroll, you will hear from him, I am sure of it."

"I'm just glad this part is over for now."

"Have a good day," she said.

My attorney was correct; as soon as the first check was garnished from his payroll, Morgan called. "Brenda, what in the hell do you think you are doing by taking $900.00 out of my paycheck every damn week?"

"Morgan, speak with my attorney."

That was the last I heard from Mr. Walsh; he wasn't hurting anyone but himself because Breanna and I will be just fine. Breanna was the best thing that had ever happened to me; I loved her more than life itself.

After picking Breanna up from the babysitter one evening, I went to the mailbox. Laying there on top of a mountain of bills, was a letter from Edgar University's

Alumni Office, which stated: "The Class of 1982 Ten Year Class Reunion." Moments later, the phone rang.

"Hey, Brenda."

"Hi, Jess. What a coincidence."

"What do you mean?" she asked.

"I just opened a letter from Edgar University regarding the reunion."

"That's why I am calling, girl. Are you going?"

"I don't know."

"Well, you should. It sounds like fun, and you need some fun in your life after all the things you've been through. A change of scenery would do you good."

"It would be nice to see the old gang and act crazy again. I can't believe it's been ten years," I said.

"I know. We are getting old."

"Speak for yourself. I'm just experienced," I said.

"I know that's right."

"Jess, I can't just jump up and take off like you, I have Breanna to consider."

"Call your mom. I am sure she wouldn't mind watching her grandbaby. I will make all the arrangements. All you have to do is show up."

"You should have majored in sales because no one can say no to you."

"I know," she said.

Thursday morning, I packed Breanna's things and took her to my mother's. Then, I came back to my place, packed a bag, jumped in my car, and was off. I arrived at the hotel for the Reunion "82." Jessica and I arrived at the same time. We checked in, got settled, and immediately started roaming the campus to see who we could find.

"Jessica, let's go over to our old hang out, Melba's Coffee House," I said.

Melba's was jumping at eleven o'clock in the morning. The aroma of grits, eggs, bacon, hash browns, and coffee filled the air.

"Girl, does this place bring back memories or what?" she said.

"You got that right, it's like we never left. Let's take a seat," I insisted.

Jessica and I sipped on coffee while going over the class reunion schedule for the weekend, not wanting to miss any events. Then, out of the blue, George and Jerry came by and sat at our table.

"Jessica, is this a bad dream?" I asked.

"Very funny."

They weren't exactly the first two people I wanted to see.

"Hello, Jessica and Brenda, it's great to see you both. You guys look great," George said.

"Isn't this strange? We met right here over ten years ago."

"It must be fate."

"Yeah, that must be it, George," I said.

"Brenda, be nice."

"Only for you, Jess. George, you look just as handsome as ever. How is your son, George Jr.?" I asked.

"He is doing well. How is your daughter, Breanna, is it?"

"Yes, that's her name, and she is wonderful, thank you."

"Why don't you both have a seat and have some breakfast with us?" Jessica said.

"George, what are you up to these days?" I asked.

"Well, I am divorced, and I'm a television anchor in Dallas, Texas. You know, I always wanted to be seen and heard."

"Yeah, that position really fits you," I said.

"Brenda, I heard you are a big-time advertising queen."

"I don't know about the queen part, but I do okay."

"Jerry, what's your story?"

"I'm single and a controller for a major fortune 500 company."

"Jessica, you and Jerry work with numbers. Interesting."

"Don't even try it, Brenda."

"I see there is a dance tonight. Would you ladies care to attend with us?"

"Yes."

"How about you, Brenda? Just a dance with no strings, I promise."

"Brenda, if you say no, I will break your neck," Jessica said.

"Easy, Jessica, I know you still have a thing for Jerry."

"Will you go?"

"As long as there are no strings," I said.

"The dance starts at nine, so we will pick you up at the hotel around nine thirty."

"Let's finish breakfast and take a stroll on campus."

"That's a good idea."

"Jessica, we need to walk this breakfast off anyway," I said.

"Hush."

While walking across campus, I heard someone call my name.

"Brenda, is that you?" It was Alfred, the first person I met when I came to Edgar University, over ten years ago.

I ran into his arms and gave him the biggest hug and kiss, ignoring the fact George was with me. "Alfred, how are you? You are still as fine as blueberry wine."

"Brenda, you have not changed a bit yourself. It is so good to see you, girl. Are you going to the dance tonight?" Alfred asked.

"Yes, Brenda is attending the dance with me. Will you be attending, Alfred?"

"Yes, I'll be there. Brenda, save a dance for me," he said.

"You know I will," I replied.

"The Alumni Ball is Saturday night. Are you booked for that evening as well?"

"No, I am not booked. I would love to attend the ball with you."

"Great, I will see you later at the dance."

By this time, it was getting late.

"Brenda and I are going to head over to the hotel. We will see you both at nine-thirty," Jess said. "Brenda, you really like Alfred, don't you?" she asked.

"You know, I can't stop thinking about him. This could be the weekend when we tell each other exactly how we feel about each other."

"I just hope you know what you are doing," Jess said.

"Me? Look at you," I replied.

"You were drooling all over Jerry today."

"All you've talked about is screwing Jerry's brains out of his head."

"Okay, what's your point?"

"Never mind, I'm getting dressed."

"I will as well. Brenda, you look fabulous. I love this little black number."

"Thank you, it's something I picked up at my favorite dress shop."

"How do I look, Brenda? Is this too much?"

"No, it's you, Jess. We are ready to party," I said.

"Brenda, was that the door?"

"Yes, I'll answer it. Hello, gentlemen. Come in. You guys look great."

"You ladies look amazing."

"Are we ready?"

"Brenda, do you have the key?" Jess asked.

"Yes, do you have yours?"

"Yes, I do."

"I guess we are ready," I said.

"This place is packed; everyone is here."

"Brenda, Jerry, and I are going to mingle," Jess said.

"Okay, I will see you in the morning," George said.

"Cute."

"Brenda, would you like to dance?" George offered.

"Yes, let's," I replied.

While I was dancing with George, I saw Alfred in the corner with some woman. Why couldn't that be me with Alfred? A real man. George noticed I was watching Alfred and purposely kept me away from him the entire evening. I was not upset because I knew our night was coming.

"Brenda, the dance is almost over; would you like to leave now?" George asked.

"Yes. Thank you very much for a lovely evening, George. Would you care to come in for coffee and conversation?"

"That would be nice."

"Come in and have a seat."

"Brenda, before we go any further, I have to apologize for misleading you when we were dating. This has been on my mind for the past ten plus years. Please, forgive me."

"I have forgiven you for quite some time now. We all make mistakes, learn from them, and move on."

"I was a fool. You are the best thing that has happened to me."

"You shouldn't feel that way George and besides, we will always be friends."

Before we knew it, it was seven o'clock in the morning and there was no sight of Jessica.

"Brenda, do you mind if I take a quick shower? Jerry and I are getting together with our fraternity brothers for breakfast."

"Sure, go right ahead. I guess that means Jessica should be coming in soon."

"Only if she doesn't find something else along the way," he said.

"That's my Jessica."

"Brenda, I am glad we had this time together so I could get these things off my chest. I feel I can move on now," he explained.

"I am glad we spoke as well, George."

"Can I see you later?"

"We will see."

"Fair enough." George left feeling really good about us.

"Where in the hell is Jessica? She should be here now. I am starving," I said to myself

I went downstairs to check my messages, and there was a note from Jessica.

Hi Brenda,

Just a quick note to inform you that I am going to have to cancel our breakfast date for this morning. Something came up. I promise to meet you at the game this afternoon.

Jessica D.

Something came up alright. It never went down. *Let me call Alfred. I am sure he would love to have breakfast with me.* To my disappointment he did not answer the telephone. *I will just go to Melba's and have breakfast alone.* No big deal. I was starving. I entered Melba's and headed for the first empty booth. A waitress came over.

"I would like a stack of blueberry pancakes, scrambled eggs, bacon, orange juice, and coffee, please."

"Sure thing, Miss."

Minutes later, my food arrived and I dug in. As I was gulping down my food, I heard a voice.

"Do you slow down to chew the food, Brenda?"

As I came up for air, I saw Alfred standing over me, laughing.

"May I have a seat?"

"Mm mm," I said.

"You and George must have had one helluva night for you to be eating like this," he commented.

"No, George and I only talked last night," I said. "I'm just hungry this morning, that's all."

"Do you remember when you first came to Edgar University and how I molded you into the beautiful woman you are today?"

"You helped mold me into a beautiful woman?" I said.

"I stand corrected. Brenda, after you eat your ten-course breakfast, would you like to spend the day with me, like ole times?"

"Yes, I thought you would never ask. Just let me go back to my room, change, and leave a note for Jessica," I said.

"Sounds good."

I went upstairs and changed into something more suitable for the occasion and ran back downstairs to the lobby. "Here I am. Where are we going, Alfred?"

"I thought we would start out with a trip to the art museum, a concert in the park, and to round it off, with going to your favorite place, the mall."

"A man after my own heart."

I felt so free and alive. Being with him was like being a kid again and not having a care in the world. We were on our way back to the hotel from an exhausting day.

"Brenda, are we still on for the alumni ball this evening?"

"Yes. Why?"

"You did have an exhausting day."

"I will be there with bells on."

"Great. I will pick you up at ten o'clock."

I went to my room to take a nap before the gala event. To my surprise, I found Jessica stretched out on the bed fast asleep. I did not wake her, as much as I wanted to. I really wanted to know what happened with her and Jerry. I took a hot shower, set the alarm for seven o'clock, and went to sleep, dreaming about Alfred. The alarm went off at seven. Jessica and I both woke up.

"Jessica, guess what: I spent the whole day with Alfred. We went to the museum, the mall, and to the park. I had a great time, and we are going to the alumni ball together."

"That's nice, Brenda, but let me tell you about my night with Jerry. Girl, we had the best sex; Jerry is still a tiger in bed. I am in love with that dick."

"Do you have to be so graphic? There's more to a man than his penis."

"Sorry, but that is all a man has to offer, and the sooner you realize that, the sooner you will stop getting hurt. Use them before they use you, girl."

"Jessica, all men aren't like that."

"Talking to you on this subject is like talking to a brick wall."

"So, are you going to the ball with Jerry tonight?"

"Yes."

I started getting ready for the ball as, Jessica continued to downgrade all men. Like clockwork, Alfred was at my door on time.

"Alfred, you look dashingly handsome in your tuxedo."

"Thank you. I have never seen you look so sexy," he said. "I love you in this gold, shimmering, strapless gown."

"I am glad you like it. I feel like Cinderella going to the ball with my prince."

"You are."

As we entered the ballroom, all eyes were on Alfred and me. We danced and held each other the entire evening, not wanting the night to end. We were dancing on air.

"Brenda, let's not allow this night to end," he whispered. "Let me take you to my room and do what I have waited ten years to do with you. Brenda, I want to make sweet, passionate love to you tonight."

I was speechless.

Alfred took me by the hand and led me out of the ballroom. There he had a bottle of champagne with two chilled glasses, strawberries, and the sounds of love-making music in the background. We drank champagne and fed each other strawberries between our long, hot kisses. I surrendered myself to Alfred. Every inch of my body was tingling with passion and excitement. We undressed each other slowly until we were totally nude. Alfred and I clutched onto each other like two wild animals in heat. Our bodies were hot like asphalt on a summer's day. He knew exactly what to do and where to touch to make my body quiver. I was in ecstasy. I felt fire in both my body and soul.

The next morning, Alfred woke me with a sensual kiss and a stack of pancakes. "Brenda, I have never felt this way before. I love you. I fell in love the first day I met you."

"Why didn't you tell me then?"

"I had a reputation back then as a 'ladies' man'. Would you have believed me if I told you years ago how I felt?"

"Probably not," I replied. "Alfred, I feel the same way as you do. I have always loved you, but I was afraid of getting hurt by you. I didn't want to destroy our great friendship either."

"I want to spend the rest of my life with you and your beautiful daughter, Breanna. Brenda, will you marry me?"

"Yes, Alfred, I will be more than happy to be your wife."

"I love you very much, and to celebrate the news, I would like for you and I to have dinner with my family tonight."

"Sweetheart, that would be lovely, but your family lives in Iowa and we are in North Carolina."

"I know, which means we can catch a flight later this morning and be there for dinner."

"That sounds great. I will call my mom and let her know I will pick up Breanna on Monday after work."

I could not wait to share the good news with Jessica, so I got dressed, grabbed my things, kissed Alfred goodbye, and ran to my room. I felt like an angel floating on a cloud. "Jess, Jess, I have the most exciting news!" I said.

"Calm down, Brenda. What is it?"

"Alfred and I are getting married!"

"Are you sure this is what you want? Don't get me wrong, I always knew one day you two would get together, but so many things have happened since the fall of 1978. People change, Brenda."

"I know, Jess. I love Alfred, and I know this is right because we became friends before lovers."

"Okay, girlfriend, you know I will be here for you."

"Does this mean you will be my maid of honor?"

"Of course. Just tell me you are not going to wear white."

"Very funny, Jess. Alfred and I are flying to Iowa later this morning to share the news with his family."

"You two really mean business."

"I will give you a call once I return to start the wedding plans. Jess, you are the best friend anyone could have, and I love you for it."

"Just be happy, girl."

Alfred and I arrived in Des Moines in no time at all. As we drove up to Alfred's parents' home, there was a feeling of family; there were homes with porches and swings and children laughing and playing, while some parents were gardening and others, barbecuing on the grill.

Alfred rang the doorbell. As the door opened, there stood his dad, mom, and two sisters with their mouths wide open.

Alfred's younger sister said, "Big brother, why is this lady with you? She is beautiful."

"Oh, be quiet, Linda. Hello, Mom and Dad. This is Brenda Peekson."

"Hello, Brenda, it is so nice to meet you, and Linda is right, you are a beautiful woman."

"Thank you, and it's nice to finally meet Alfred's family. He speaks very highly of you all."

"Come on in and take a load off. Alfred, take Brenda's bags to the guest room."

"So, Alfred, what's the big news you have to tell us?"

"Dad, I will tell the family during dinner."

"Come on, the suspense is killing us."

"Okay."

"Dad, Mom, Kate, and Linda, Brenda and I are engaged to be married."

"Congratulations, my son! I am so proud of you and Brenda. Now, let's celebrate. Honey, I will get a bottle of our best champagne."

"Honey, it's our only bottle of champagne."

"This news is worth opening it."

Alfred's family was very happy for us. We had a lovely dinner and hopped on a plane back to North Carolina. The next several weeks were hectic with work and planning yet another wedding (I was getting really good at this). I promised myself this wedding will be small and private; family only, with the exception of Jessica, of course. I felt, at last, I was making the right decision regarding spending the rest of my life with Alfred. He was so warm, honest, understanding, caring, sweet, lovable, and he loved Breanna.

Chapter Five

Returning home from a business trip in Washington, DC, Alfred picked me up at the airport in a black limousine with a bouquet of my favorite tulips in his hands.

"Baby, I am so glad to see you. I missed you so much, Brenda."

"I missed you too, babe. What is the occasion?"

"I have some exciting news that's going to change our lives."

"Sweetie, what is it?"

"Here it goes: Brenda, you are looking at the newest Principal of Robotics Engineering."

"Alfred, this is great news! I'm so happy for you, but I didn't know you were even considering this position."

"I wanted to surprise you with the good news if I got the position, and if I didn't get it, I didn't want to disappoint you and Breanna."

"Alfred, don't be silly, you could never disappoint us."

"Thank you, baby."

"Now, with this new position, I can afford to give you and Breanna the kind of life we deserve."

"What do you mean, Alfred?"

"I just mean we can have a beautiful house on Lakeview Lane. You can quit your job for a while and we can start planning our family like we have discussed."

"This is amazing, but I am not ready to add to our family now."

"I know. What I'm saying is the world is your oyster, and when you want to put your career on hold and start adding to our family, we wouldn't have to worry about income because I will make enough money for the both of us. That's all, honey, just think about it."

"Okay."

The next morning, Jessica called to remind me she was in town and coming over to go shopping. When Jessica arrived, we went into the kitchen to have coffee and donuts.

"So, how are things going?" Jessica asked.

"Crazy."

"What do you mean? Breanna's father hasn't been bothering you, has he?"

"No, Jess, that's all I need. I have been traveling more than ever for work and planning a wedding, which is very stressful."

"Is that it, Brenda? Because you are a very strong person and can handle anything."

"Well. Now that you mention it, Alfred said something last week that kind of bothers me."

"What?"

"Alfred has a new job as the Principal of Robotics Engineering."

"That's great news, Brenda. What's the problem?"

"Well, with this new position, Alfred will be making a great deal more money, and he said, in so many words, he wants me to quit my job and stay home at our new place on Lakeview Lane and have babies."

"Brenda, here we go again. What in the hell is your problem? This man loves you and wants to give you the world."

"Why can't I be so lucky?"

"Brenda, get over it. Alfred doesn't want to control you like you think, he just wants you to be happy and stress-free. He worships the ground you and Breanna walk on. He even wants to adopt Breanna. How many men do you know would love you enough to adopt your child as his own? You should drop to your knees every night, girl, and thank God for Alfred."

"Maybe you are right, Jess."

"I know I'm right. Stop looking for trouble, and let's go shopping for that wedding dress."

Alfred kept his word and we moved to a giant home on Lakeview Lane. It was a beautiful seven-bedroom house with a huge deck and an apartment on the grounds for our family members when they come to visit. Instead of having a church wedding, Alfred and I decided to have our wedding ceremony and reception at our new home.

The big day arrived, and even though I had been through it before, I still was nervous. But Jessica was there holding my hand every step of the way. The wedding was picture-perfect. Breanna looked adorable in her pink laced flower girl's dress. Alfred stood there so handsome in his sapphire silk suit, waiting for his wife-to-be. I wore an ivory, chiffon layered, floor length dress. Things were going great with my new role as a housewife. For the first time in a long time, we all had breakfast at the table.

Alfred kissed me and Breanna good-bye and went on his way to work as I cleaned Breanna up and took her to kindergarten. At night, we had dinner together, as opposed to going out, because now I had time to cook.

One afternoon, as I was watching videos with Breanna, the telephone rang.

"Hey, old married lady, what's happening?" Jessica asked.

"Jessica, long time no hear. I thought you'd forgotten about your best friend," I said.

"Never Brenda, I just wanted to give you and that new hubby of yours time to yourselves."

"Well, there has been a lot of changes for me here."

"Me too girl, that's one of the reasons I'm calling you. You go first, Brenda."

"I am no longer a career woman. I was laid off from the agency. (Alfred got his wish) I'm a housewife and I love it."

"This is great news because I am being transferred to North Carolina. My company has opened an accounting firm there and I'll be heading the office."

"Go on with your bad self. I can't wait. When are you coming? Do you have a place to stay?" I asked.

"Slow down, Brenda. I will be there in a couple days to look for a place."

"Don't be silly; you can stay with us. We have this huge house equipped with everything."

"Girl, I don't want to impose."

"You wouldn't be imposing, you could stay in the apartment."

"Shouldn't you pass this by Alfred first?"

"We'd both be more than happy to have you stay here for as long as you want," I insisted.

"Well, I guess it's settled. I will see you guys in a few days," she said.

"I can't wait to see you."

Just as I thought, Alfred had no problem with Jessica visiting with us; he only wanted me to be happy. Jessica and I were like two college kids again, staying up all night, especially when Alfred was out of town, munching on popcorn, pizza, nachos, and soda pop, laughing, and talking about the past and how we ever survived it.

Things were going well for a while, and I began acting moody. And everyone noticed it.

"Brenda, honey, are you alright? I have noticed you haven't been yourself lately." Alfred said.

"I am sorry babe. I don't know what's wrong with me, but I have been feeling edgy."

"I know you loved working. Maybe you're a little bored, and it would be great if the economy would get better. But, in the meantime, it would be a good idea if you looked into joining some social organization to get more involved in the community and volunteer your services. I remembered, when we were in college, you loved that stuff."

"I do need to get my juices flowing again, and this just might be the ticket," I said. "I will look into some of the local clubs in the area, and maybe Jessica would like to join as well."

"Jess is pretty busy with her job, Brenda."

"I know, but it won't hurt to ask." I rarely saw Jess anymore because she was so busy, and I thought she was seeing a man, even though she denied it.

Alfred's suggestion was a good one; I joined a woman's group and was on the board at the chamber of commerce. I felt great now that I was back in the thick of things, networking and mingling. Things were better at home as well. Alfred and I went to bed earlier and earlier, and we weren't sleeping.

"Well, hello there, stranger. Long time no see. If I didn't know you any better, I would think you were trying to avoid me," I said.

"I know, and I am sorry, Brenda," Jessica replied.

"Don't worry about it. I am not your mother. You can come and go as you please, but I would like to catch up with you and chat. Let's do dinner Saturday at six right here on the deck."

"It's a date. Are you okay?"

"Yes, why?"

"You look weak."

"I am a little tired, but that's it."

"If you say so, buddy. Oh, by the way, here's the mail."

"Thanks, Jess." I looked down at the mail and my eyes widened.

"Brenda, what's wrong? You look like you just saw a ghost or something."

"Worse, it's a letter from Morgan, Breanna's father."

"What in the hell does he want? He hasn't contacted you in years. Open it and read the letter."

"I am scared."

"I'll read it."

"No, just give me a minute, Jess."

It said:

Dear Brenda,

I am sure this letter comes as a surprise to you, considering you haven't heard from me in three years. I certainly hope you and Breanna are doing well. I'm sure she's a big girl now.

The reason I am writing to you now is I want to spend more time with you and Breanna. It took me three years to finally realize how much of a fool I've been and what I've missed out on not being with the both of you. I just hope it's not too late.

I truly care about you and Breanna, and I also want my daughter to know her biological father. I know I have been a jerk in the past, but now I've matured and know what's important to me, and that's you and Breanna.

I know all the hurt I have caused in the past won't disappear after you read this letter, but could you at least give me a second chance? I promise to make it up to you. I am not expecting you to come to any decision right away, but when you do, please contact me.

Love,
Morgan Walsh

"The nerve of him. I can't believe this guy. He wants you to forget what he put you through, especially when you were pregnant," Jess said.

"I know, and feel the same way, but he is Breanna's father, Jess."

"What are you saying, Brenda?"

"I'm saying I don't want a future with Morgan. I'm not stupid, but I do want Breanna to know her father."

"I hope you're going to discuss this with Alfred. Doesn't Morgan know you are married?"

"He should, unless he's been living under a rock, because the wedding announcement was in every newspaper in North Carolina."

"I don't know about this, Brenda. I think if you allow Morgan to see Breanna, it's only going to cause problems for you and Alfred."

"Alfred is a very secure man, Jess, and I don't see him being threatened by Morgan."

"Oh, come on, haven't I taught you anything? All men are insecure when it comes to other men around their women, especially if you and the other man have a past like you and Morgan."

"I'll bring this up with Alfred after dinner tonight."

"Thanks for the warning; I'll eat out tonight."

"I'm going to pick Breanna up from school. I will see you Saturday for dinner."

"Okay, see ya."

• • • • •

"Hi, sweetheart, this house smells like Christmas dinner. What's the occasion?" Alfred asked while walking through the door.

"I just wanted to make a special dinner for my wonderful family."

"I am ready, let's dig in."

"So, how was your day at the office, babe?"

"Busy. We are introducing a new system next week, and fortunately we found a malfunction in it before going public. What happened around here today?"

"Jessica stopped by, we chatted over coffee, and I received an interesting letter in the mail."

"From who?"

"Morgan, Breanna's father."

"What did he say?"

"He apologized for being an absentee father and now wants to make up for it by spending more time with Breanna."

"Does he want anything from you?"

"He wants a rekindling of our relationship."

"It's obvious he doesn't know you are now happily married."

"No, I don't think so."

"Brenda, what are you going to do?"

"I'd like to give him a chance to prove to me he is sincere about being a father to Breanna by having supervised visits with you and me."

"Brenda, he acted as if Breanna didn't exist for years, and now, all of a sudden, he wants to play daddy. I don't trust this guy, and, besides, you could say, because he does not have a leg to stand on, he has no parental rights."

"I'm not looking at this from a legal point, but from a parent/child point. I don't want Breanna to grow up thinking I kept her and her father apart. You understand that, don't you?"

"Yes, I understand your position in all this, and I sympathize with you, honey. I just don't trust the man."

"Can we at least give Morgan the benefit of the doubt?"

"One chance, and one chance only. I'm not putting up with any of his bullshit."

"I agree with you, and I will call Morgan first thing in the morning."

"Enough about Morgan. I would like to take my two favorite girls out for ice cream."

As promised, the next day I called Morgan at his office. He was not in, so I left a message.

Three days later, Morgan returned my call. This was not a good sign. "Hello, Brenda, sorry it took me so long to get back to you."

"Good day, Morgan, the reason I called you was in response to your letter. There are a few things we need to discuss."

"Slow down, Brenda, this isn't a conference call. You don't have to be so formal and businesslike. How is my daughter?"

"Breanna is fine, and this is business, Morgan. There have been some major changes in our lives. My name is now Brenda Peekson Holmes. I am married to a wonderful man who loves me and Breanna very much. We both discussed your request to re-enter Breanna's life and agreed it would be good for Breanna to establish a relationship with her biological father. In the beginning, your visits will be here at my home, supervised by my husband, Alfred, and I. Once you have proven yourself, you then will be able to take Breanna to the park, museum, movies, etc."

"Brenda, how long have you been married to Mr. Holmes?"

"Two years."

"I guess this means there is no hope for you and me."

"Correct, Morgan. You can have a relationship with your daughter, but I don't want a relationship with you. The only reason I'm speaking with you now is because of Breanna. You can visit Breanna every other weekend at 2:00 p.m. for a couple of hours, starting next week."

"I really wanted to have another chance with you, Brenda."

"You ran out of chances when you ran out on me when I needed you most."

"I'll come to see my daughter at the scheduled time. What is your address?"

"1734 Lakeview Lane."

"Well, at least you married money."

"Goodbye, Morgan."

How and why did I ever get involved with that man? I asked myself.

I cleaned Breanna up Saturday afternoon for her visit with her father. Alfred was even a little curious in meeting Morgan. I guess he either wanted to see what kind of a man I was attracted to, or compare himself with him. When two o'clock came, there was no Morgan. Three o'clock, no Morgan, and at this point, I became very upset and disappointed for Breanna.

"Brenda, we have waited long enough for Mr. Irresponsible. Why does this not surprise me?"

"Go ahead and say it, Alfred."

"Say what?"

"I told you so."

"Sweetheart, I would never say such a thing because I love you and Breanna."

"Thank you, honey. I needed to hear that. I'm just glad Breanna isn't old enough to understand what's going on."

"After today, I am surer than ever, that I want to adopt Breanna. If it's okay with you, I would like to call my attorney tomorrow and have him draw up the papers to get the process started."

"Alfred, I don't deserve you."

"We deserve each other."

"I'll take Breanna upstairs to change her clothes, then I'll start dinner. Remember, Jessica is coming over tonight."

"That's right. Would you mind if I don't stay around for dinner? I have a lot of work to do, which I didn't get a chance to complete earlier today."

"Could you hang around long enough for a drink with us?"

"Sure, and I will put some steaks and burgers on the grill."

"You are amazing."

"Knock, knock, can I come in?" It was Jessica.

"Hey, girl, come on in. We are out on the deck. I have a drink with your name on it."

"Those steaks smell great, Alfred."

"Thanks, Jess, how have you been?" Alfred asked.

"Very good, just busy. There's a lot of responsibility that comes with heading an office, but you know that."

"Yes, I do. Unfortunately, I won't be able to join you guys for dinner because my desk is full of work I have to complete by Monday."

"That's too bad."

"I have been working so much, I haven't had a chance to date anyone, and you know me, Brenda, I need a man in my life," Jessica said.

"I thought you were seeing someone, Jess?"

"He was just a free meal; there was no attraction at all."

"Oh, Jess."

"Brenda, you are getting yours every night, so don't say a word."

"Eat, Jessica."

"How's my favorite little angel today, Breanna?"

"Pumpkin is doing fine."

"How did the visit go today?"

"I will tell you about it later."

"Well, I am going to tackle my desk in the study. You two have a great visit. It was good to see you again, and don't be a stranger, Jessica," Alfred said.

"It was good to see you too, Alfred," Jessica replied.

"See you later, baby."

"Once again, I ask you, Brenda, how did you get so lucky? Alfred is the sweetest guy I know."

"It's true; I am a lucky woman and I thank God for my life every day," I said.

"So, tell me, how was Morgan's visit today?"

"You wouldn't believe it, Morgan didn't show up."

"Did he call?"

"No."

"What?"

"I don't believe this asshole. He was the one who wrote this lovely letter, saying he wants to be a part of his daughter's life, and then he doesn't show up to see Breanna. What a jerk."

"I am sorry, Brenda, but this only shows he doesn't give a damn about her. You should just accept the fact he is a loser and move on."

"I have. We gave him a chance to prove himself and he blew it. Alfred has a meeting with his attorney to begin the process of adoption. He wants more than ever to be Breanna's legal father."

"That's great, Brenda. I am very happy for you. Do you think Morgan will sign the papers for this?"

"Yes, because it's obvious he doesn't care about Breanna, and the fact he wouldn't have to pay child support anymore should be enough for him to be more than happy to sign the papers. Just look at his track record."

"I agree with you, but Morgan does a lot of things to annoy and frustrate you, anything to prolong the process. All I am saying is keep your guard up."

"We will."

"And, if there is anything I can do, like hire a few people to take Morgan out of his misery, please let me know."

"Thanks, Jess."

Weeks later, our attorney put the adoption process in motion. He did not foresee any problem, just as we thought. He basically said if everything continued to go smoothly, the adoption would be finalized by Christmas. That would be the best gift ever for our family. In the meantime, we just waited.

Alfred was quickly moving up in the company, promotion after promotion came his way, and needless to say, he was on top of the world. He was also working longer hours. I assumed by being a principal Alfred would delegate duties, but knowing Alfred like I do, he always had to be on top of things.

"Hello, sweetie," said Alfred.

"You surprised me. Why are you home so early?" I asked.

"Is it wrong for me to want to spend the afternoon with my beautiful and sexy wife?"

"Keep talking, baby."

"I want to make hot and passionate love to you in every room of this house again."

"Alfred, what's gotten into you?"

"I know I have been neglecting you and Breanna lately, so, starting now, that will change."

"What do you mean?" I asked.

"I plan to spend more time with you and show you how much you mean to me."

"Oh, Alfred."

"I also have another surprise for you," he said.

"What is it?"

"I will tell you after dinner at your favorite restaurant."

"You mean my absolute very favorite restaurant, the V. R.?"

"Yes, baby, I made reservations for tonight at seven."

"Who is going to watch Breanna?" I inquired.

"Jessica has volunteered to pick Breanna up from school, as well as babysit tonight."

"You have thought of everything, Mr. Holmes."

"And now my mind is on one thing. We have a lot of rooms to get to by seven."

"Lead the way."

Alfred and I were in our own little world and we didn't hear Jessica ringing the doorbell.

"Will someone open the door? It's cold out here!" Jessica yelled.

"Just a second, Jess."

"Come on!" she yelled.

"We are coming!"

"It's about time. What were you two doing? Don't answer that," Jessica retorted.

"Hi, Breanna, how is mommy and daddy's little girl?" I asked.

"Do you realize it is six o'clock?" Jessica mentioned.

"Oh my God, we have to get dressed!" I exclaimed.

Jessica took Brenna into the kitchen. "Okay, Breanna, let's see what we can put together for dinner."

One hour later...

"Alfred, this place is just as I remembered, plush and elegant," I said.

"The V.R. can't hold a candle to you, my dear. You are so beautiful."

"Thank you, honey. I feel like this is a dream and you are my prince."

"It's no dream, baby, and I am your prince forever. Brenda, our wedding anniversary is coming up soon and I want us to do something special this year."

"What do you have in mind, babe?"

"Open this," he requested.

"Two roundtrip tickets to Paris, Italy, and Germany! Oh, Alfred!"

"Just you and me in Europe for a month. How does that sound? Alfred asked.

"It sounds heavenly. I have the best husband in the world."

"And I have the best wife. I love you, Brenda."

Chapter Six

Our trip was breathtaking. Alfred and I rekindled our love under the moonlit, romantic skies of Europe. We returned home, floating on a cloud. Things were heavenly. I could have stayed in Europe forever if Breanna was with us, but it was also good to come home to reality.

Alfred was back hard at work, while I was handling the home front. One afternoon while I was cleaning Breanna's room, the telephone rang; it was Alfred's attorney.

"Hello, Brenda, is Alfred there?"

"Yes, he is."

"Could he pick up on another line? I want you both to hear the news."

"Alfred, honey, pick up the phone."

"Hi, what's up?"

"Brenda, Alfred, the reason I wanted the both of you on the telephone is to let you know Morgan has signed the right to waive his parental obligations, which means this gives you the green light to adopt Breanna."

"What do we do next?"

"I have set a court date for Tuesday morning at 11:00 a.m. for you and Brenda to come before the judge, which is a formality. He will ask you basic questions like; do you agree and understand the adoption procedure? Will you follow the rules and obligations of being a parent? Also, do you love the child? Simple questions like that. You will also sign adoption papers stating you are Breanna's legal father."

"This is great news."

"I will see you both in court on Tuesday."

Everything went smoothly, just as our attorney said it would. We came before the judge. He asked both of us questions and granted Alfred the legal adoption. It took only fifteen minutes. After thanking the judge and our attorney, Alfred, Breanna, and I celebrated with lunch at Breanna's favorite hamburger restaurant.

That night, we invited over a few close friends and family to celebrate the good news. Breanna asked Alfred if she could call him daddy, which brought tears to my eyes as Alfred said yes. We were the perfect little family.

The next day, as I was relaxing on the deck, the telephone rang. It was Alfred.

"Hey, honey, what's cooking?"

"Nothing much, babe. I was just sitting here on the deck reading a magazine and thinking to myself it was almost time for me to take Breanna to her annual medical checkup."

"I can't believe our baby girl will soon be four years old."

"I know, where does the time go? As long as I'll be at the doctor's office, I'll also see the doctor myself."

"What's wrong, Brenda? Are you okay?"

"Yes, I feel fine. It's just a routine checkup, that's all."

"You would tell me if there was something wrong, wouldn't you?"

"Of course, Alfred."

"I'll be home by six tonight. Love you."

"Love you too. See you then."

I got Breanna to the doctor on time where she was found to be in perfect health.

Now it was my turn. The nurse volunteered to watch Breanna while I saw my doctor. He gave a basic checkup. He took my blood, urine, checked my heart, lungs, and weight. He told me everything looks good, but if something should come up in the tests, he would call me. Breanna and I stopped by a restaurant to have a snack before heading home. As we entered the house, the telephone was ringing; it was my doctor.

"Good evening, Mrs. Holmes. I'm sorry for calling so late, but I thought you would want to know the results of your test."

"Yes, of course, doctor."

"Brenda, according to the test results, you are about seven weeks pregnant."

"I am?"

"Yes, you are. Congratulations to you and Mr. Holmes."

"Thank you so much."

"I want you to call next week to set up prenatal visits."

"I will, and thanks again."

Alfred will be so happy to learn he will be a biological dad at last. I couldn't wait until he came home to share the good news. In the meantime, I put Breanna down for the night and began to prepare a special dinner for us.

Alfred came home with a bouquet of flowers in one hand and a stuffed animal in the other.

"Hi, sweetie, what's all this?"

"Just a small token of love for my favorite girls."

"Thank you, honey. You are so thoughtful."

"Let's eat. Brenda, this steak is amazing; it melts in your mouth. What is your secret?"

"Love, pure love."

"Thank you for a wonderful meal, Brenda. I will clean up the kitchen, and you can just relax."

"It's a deal."

"So, how was your day? What did the doctor say?"

"Funny you should ask. Breanna is doing great; she is a healthy four-year-old."

"And how was your checkup?"

"Honey, I have been waiting all night for this moment. Alfred, we are going to have a baby."

"A baby, you're pregnant?"

"Yes, we are pregnant."

"Oh, Brenda, you have made me the luckiest man in the world! How pregnant are we?"

"Seven weeks."

"I love you, Brenda."

"I love you too, Alfred."

"I want you to be careful and not to overexert yourself. We can get a nanny/housekeeper to help out. I want you to have a wonderful pregnancy."

"That would be nice."

"Have you told anyone yet?"

"No, you are the first."

"Let's share the news with our parents, starting with yours," Albert said.

Our parents were ecstatic with joy and happiness, especially Alfred's parents because this will be their first grandchild.

Alfred treated me like a queen of queens; I didn't think things could have gotten better, but they did. I did not lift a finger. Alfred hired a housekeeper and a nanny to take care of things for me while I concentrated on having a perfect pregnancy.

Jessica became my eating partner. We went to every restaurant in town that offered an "All you can eat buffet." They knew us by name. "Brenda, are you always hungry? Because you're eating like you haven't seen food in years," Jessica said.

"No, it's just that I'm using this pregnancy as an excuse to stuff my face. What about you? You are putting your share away as well."

"After the baby is born, I will get back to my exercise routine, I promise. And you should join me."

"Okay," Jess said.

I was eight and a half months pregnant, and going to the doctor every week with my Alfred right there with me every step of the way. At this particular visit, I was given an ultrasound to see the baby's position. Also, we got a chance to see the sex of our child.

"Mr. and Mrs. Holmes, I can tell you the sex of your baby, if you want to know?"

"Honey, do you want to know?" Albert asked.

"Yes," I replied.

"Me too."

"It looks you will be having a baby boy," the doctor informed us.

"Thank you, Brenda, thank you, thank you, for giving me a son!"

"No, thank you," I replied. "Alfred, could you please make an appointment with the doctor for yourself? Babe, you've been complaining about your body aching, and you are looking a bit tired lately. You are always taking care of everyone else and not yourself. Remember, this little boy I'm carrying is going to need you to teach him how to be a man and do all of the wonderful things fathers and sons do."

"Babe, I will make an appointment before leaving this building, I promise."

• • • • •

The doctor couldn't see Alfred for an entire month; he was booked. Even though I would've liked it to have been sooner, I guess it could've been worse, two months instead of one. Now we were coming down to the wire. I began having Braxton Hicks contractions two weeks before my due date, and Alfred insisted on staying home with me, which was nice to having him around during the day. One day, Alfred had to go into the office for a few hours, and I reassured him I would be alright.

While Alfred was at work, I decided to take a long and relaxing hot bath. As I was coming out of the bathtub, my water broke, labor pains started, and they were worse than when I was in labor with Breanna. I screamed out to my housekeeper Maria and asked her to call Alfred and have him meet me at the hospital, call 911, and call Jessica. It figures the day Alfred wasn't here, I would go into labor. The ambulance arrived and rushed me to the hospital where Alfred and Jessica were impatiently waiting.

"Brenda, how are you feeling?"

"Not too good, Alfred. This little boy wants to come out now."

"Hey, girl, I am here for you," Jessica said.

"Thanks for being here, Jessica."

"Hi, Mr. and Mrs. Holmes, I understand we are going to have a baby today," Dr. Perez announced while entering.

"Oh, yes, we are Dr. Perez."

"Let me check to see how far you have dilated. Brenda, this baby needs a haircut. He has a lot of hair on his head, and you have dilated nine centimeters, which means it's time to push."

"Honey, I love you and I am here for you."

"I love you too, Alfred."

"Brenda, you know the routine. Push only when I tell you to, and continue to breathe. Push. That's was a good one; I see the head."

"Alfred, did you hear that? The doctor can see our son's head."

"Honey, I can see him. He does have a lot of hair."

"Brenda, I know you have the urge to push, but don't," cautioned Dr. Perez.

"I can't help it, doctor!"

"Brenda, it's almost over. Just two more good pushes should do it. You are doing great."

"Honey, listen to Dr. Perez," Albert said.

"Alfred, you don't have this baby in you. It hurts!"

"Get ready to push again. Sit up and push. Good, good, here comes his shoulders. Stop pushing, relax for a minute. You are coming down to the wire, Brenda.

Okay, this is it, push! Keep pushing, here he comes. Congratulations, you are the proud parents of a little boy," said Dr. Perez.

"Alfred, would you like to cut the umbilical cord?"

"Yes, I would."

"Don't be nervous, honey; it's okay."

"Brenda, the doctor is right; our son is beautiful."

"Can I hold my baby now?"

"Yes, ma'am."

"Brenda, you did a great job and thank you."

"Alfred, we haven't decided on a name yet."

"What do you want to name our bundle of joy?"

"I want you to name him."

"I would love to name him, Alfred Brandon Holmes II."

"It's perfect."

"Mrs. Holmes, the nurse needs to clean the baby and take him to the nursery; she will bring him back later. In the meantime, we will take you to your room."

"Alfred, can you tell Jess that we have a son and I want to see her?"

"Of course. Honey, is there anything special you would like to eat?"

"Yes, some roasted chicken with all the trimmings."

"I will be back soon."

"I love you, baby."

Alfred walked out into the waiting room where he found Jess pacing back and forth.

"Alfred, how is Brenda?" Jess, asked.

"Brenda and Alfred Brandon Holmes II are doing just fine; she wants to see you now," Alfred said.

"Where are you going?"

"To make some calls and to get Brenda some food."

"At least she didn't lose her appetite. Hi there, Momma, how are you feeling?"

"Hi, Jess. Happy, tired and sore."

"I stopped by the nursery. He is simply breathtaking. I am so happy for you and Alfred."

"Thank you, and also thank you for being here with us all night."

"Is there anything you need?" Jess asked.

"No, I am all set."

"I see Alfred is on a food run for you."

"Don't start."

"I'm not. This is your day, you deserve it. I am going to go home and check on things and take a nap as well. I love you."

"I love you too, Jess."

Alfred came back with Breanna to see her new baby brother. We all had dinner together. After dinner, Alfred took Breanna home and returned to spend the night with little Alfred and me.

Later that evening, the nurse came in to inform us since everything went well, I could go home the next day, which was good news because I couldn't wait to begin enjoying my family.

In the beginning, like most newborn babies, little Alfred was up all night. But, in time, he slept more at night. Breanna was also happy being a big sister to her little brother. Everyone was doing fine and adjusting well to the new addition, except Alfred. One morning during breakfast, Alfred excused himself four times from the table.

"Alfred, is everything alright?" I asked.

"Yes, why you ask?"

"Honey, you've left the table four times."

"I just went to the bathroom."

"You went to the bathroom four times. That's not normal. Have you seen the doctor yet?"

"I cancelled that appointment, Brenda."

"What?"

"I had to cancel my appointment with the doctor because the CEO came to town and wanted to meet with all principals on that day, and besides, I feel fine," he assured.

"You can't be feeling fine if you're using the bathroom four times in less than ten minutes. Are you experiencing any pain?"

"A little."

"You need to see a doctor ASAP."

"Brenda, you are making this a big deal and it's not."

"Big deal or not, Alfred, I love you too much, and I am going to call Dr. Walden."

"You are upsetting Breanna," he said as Breanna began to cry.

"Breanna, Mommy and Daddy are having a conversation. Calm down, sweetie. Everything is fine. I will call Dr. Walden first thing in the morning."

• • • • •

The next day, Brenda made time to call the doctor.

The secretary answered, "Hello, Dr. Walden's office."

"Good day, this is Brenda Holmes and I would like to reschedule an appointment for my husband, Alfred, to see the doctor. He is urinating more than normal."

"It just so happens there was a cancellation for 11:30 today."

"11:30 is good. We will be there," Brenda replied and hung up the phone. "Honey, the doctor will see you today at 11:30 a.m., and I am going with you."

"Brenda, do you not trust me?"

"Not on this one, Alfred. Let's go."

As soon as we arrived, Alfred was escorted back to the examining room. I read every magazine and newspaper while waiting for Alfred to return. Two hours past, and still no Alfred. I became really worried and asked the medical assistant at the front desk to see if she could find   out what was going on. She came back to say, someone will be out shortly.

Twenty minutes later, Dr. Walden enters the waiting area. "Brenda, can you come with me?"

"Is everything alright? Where is Alfred?"

"I have admitted Alfred into the hospital."

"Why, what's wrong?"

"After examining Alfred, I gave him a PSA, prostate specific antigen test and a MRI. The results show that Alfred has at least two aggressive tumors on his prostate, and it looks as if it could have spread into his lymph nodes."

"Are the tumors cancerous?"

"I am not sure, Brenda."

"How did this happen? Alfred has always been so strong and healthy. Will he be alright?"

"I would like to do a biopsy and operate, in order to take the tumors out. After the biopsy, we will know if the tumors are malignant or benign. For now, I need for you to sign some papers as we get Alfred prepped for surgery."

"Of course, doctor. Can I see him? I want Alfred to know I am here and love him very much."

"Yes, but only for a few minutes."

"Thank you, doctor."

"Brenda, I will do everything in my power for Alfred. I will see you after the surgery."

"Thank you so much, doctor."

As I entered Alfred's room, there were nurses prepping him for surgery with intravenous needles in his arms and tubes in his nose. I kept saying to myself, *Brenda, you have to be strong, for yourself and Alfred.*

"Hello, sunshine, how's the love of my life?"

"Brenda, I thought I was coming in today to get a routine checkup, and now I'm being prepped for surgery."

"You know, it's never a dull moment with us," I said.

"Seriously, has the doctor explained to you what's going on? Did you know it looks like I may have prostate cancer?"

"Nothing has been confirmed; the tumors could be benign," I said.

"And they could also very well be malignant. Brenda, I just want you to be prepared for the worst."

"Thank you, honey, but at this time, I'd rather stay positive."

"Alfred, it's time to go," the doctor interrupted.

"Sweetie, I will be right here when you come out of surgery," Brenda reassured.

"I love you, babe."

"I love you too."

"Brenda, could you call my office and let them know I won't be in for a few days or so?"

"Will do, and I will call your family as well."

"I don't want them to worry. Please don't call them until there is reason to."

"Okay, I will call your office."

As Alfred was being wheeled into surgery, I kept saying to myself, *God, please don't take Alfred away from me.* I called my home and told Maria, the nanny I would be home late. I called Alfred's office as well, to inform them Alfred would be out for a couple of days. I knew Alfred didn't want anyone to know, but I had to talk to Jessica before I went crazy.

"Hello, Jess? I need you. I am at the hospital."

"Brenda, what's wrong? Are you and the kids alright?"

"It's Alfred; he went to the doctor this morning for a physical. They found tumors on his prostate and lymph nodes, and now he's in surgery getting the tumors removed. And then they will do a biopsy."

"Brenda, everything will be fine."

"I hope so, Jess. I lost Robert, and I just can't deal with losing Alfred too."

"Where are the kids?"

"They are home with the nanny, and I am here alone because Alfred doesn't want anyone to know right now, but I had to call you."

"I'm on my way. Hang in there," Jessica said.

"I will try, and in the meantime, I am going to be in the chapel."

"See you soon."

I didn't attend church often, but I believed in God. As I entered the empty chapel, I felt a sense of warmth and comfort. I prayed:

Dear Lord,

I know it seems as if I only come to you when my life is in an uproar, but I come to you today as a child of God. You are an all-knowing and Almighty God, and right now, my husband is in surgery having tumors removed. God, please help make Alfred well again. After I lost Robert, I did not ever think I could love again, and then you brought Alfred back into my life. I became whole again, and we are blessed with two beautiful children. Lord, I know you don't give any more than one can handle, but I can't handle any more. Please, God, make those tumors in Alfred's body not cancerous. This I ask in the name of Jesus Christ. Amen.

As I left the chapel, I saw Jessica walking down the hall.

"Hi Brenda, I got here as soon as I could. Is there any word?"

"No, nothing yet. I am glad you're here."

"I brought you something to eat."

"Jess, I won't be able to eat a thing until I know Alfred is okay."

"Brenda, were there any symptoms?"

"The only thing I know is the prostate is a gland that manufactures the liquid ejaculate that carries sperm out of the body. As far as the symptoms are concerned, Alfred never said a word, but at breakfast he went to the bathroom four times in less than ten minutes. That's when I called the doctor, and now he is in the operating room. But, from what I understand, the symptoms are frequent and painful urination, and sometimes it can cause blood in the urine as well. And Alfred never said a word."

"Really, not one word, Brenda?"

"Nope, nothing. You know Alfred, 'The Almighty Protector" of the family. He didn't want me to worry. I need Alfred. I can't lose him. Why is this happening to me? What have I done? Jessica, Alfred will be fine. I just know it. Here comes Alfred's doctor."

"Hi Brenda, I found more tumors on Alfred's prostate and in his lymph nodes."

"Did you get them all?"

"We removed what we could see."

"How is he?" I asked.

"He came through surgery fine and is now in recovery."

"What's the next step, doctor?" Jessica asked.

"I'm sorry, this is my best friend, Jessica," I explained.

"Now the tumors are on their way to the lab for tests."

"How long will that take?" I asked.

"I put a rush on them, which means I should get the results within twenty-four hours, at the latest, but I want to keep him here overnight for observation."

"Can I see him now?"

"Yes, but he may be a little woozy."

"I won't be long."

"Brenda, go on. I will be here waiting," Jess said.

"Thank you." I walked into Alfred's room. "Hi, big guy, how do you feel?" I asked.

"Like I am floating on cloud nine, feeling no pain. Am I okay?"

"Dr. Walden removed all the tumors and put a rush for the lab to send him the results."

"Will I live?"

"Of course you will live, Alfred."

"Good. You should go home to the children and get some rest yourself."

"Honey, I will be fine," I said. "If you say so, babe, but I'll be back first thing in the morning. We can have breakfast together. Do you need anything? Are you in pain? Should I call the nurse?"

"Honey, I am fine. Go home and get some rest. You worry too much."

"I am a wife and a mother, it's my job to worry. See you in the morning. I love you, Alfred."

"I love you more, Brenda."

Brenda walked out to the waiting room where Jess was sitting.

"How is he?" Jess asked.

"Alfred is okay. He is still a little out of it and sleepy. He told me to go home to get some rest."

"That's a great idea. I will take you home."

"That's okay, I have my car in the garage," I said.

"Just leave it there until tomorrow, because you are not in any condition to drive alone."

"You're right."

Jessica drove me towards my house. On the way, I couldn't shake the feeling this was happening for a reason.

"Jess, do you think I'm a bad person?"

"Of course not."

"Well then, why are we going through this?"

"Brenda, you are a strong woman."

"I'm tired of being strong."

"I know, but everything is going to be alright."

"Here we are."

We arrived home.

"Jess, can you please come in with me for a while?"

"I plan to."

We entered my house to find Maria in the kitchen. She had been kind enough to stay with the kids while I was at the hospital.

"Hi, Maria, how are my bundles of joy?" I asked.

"They are fine. I gave them dinner and their baths, and now they are both tucked away in bed. Should I prepare a late dinner for you and Ms. Jessica?"

"No, that will be all for tonight, Maria."

"Goodnight, madam."

"Goodnight, Maria."

"Brenda, you should go upstairs and take a long hot bath while I make coffee and a couple of sandwiches."

"That sounds like a great idea."

I went upstairs, checked in on my little angels, gave them a kiss, and hopped into an inviting bubble bath. A bath was just what I needed. As I slipped into the hot and steamy tub, the water soothing my tired body. I closed my eyes and felt as if I drifted off into another world; and all of my worries were behind me.

"Brenda, are you okay?" Jess asked through the door. "You've been in the tub for two hours."

"I am fine, Jess. I'll be down in a minute."

"Girl, you should be a raisin by now, for as long as you have been in that tub."

"I didn't realize I was in the tub for that long. I am sorry."

"Don't be silly, I just wanted to make sure you were okay. Eat your sandwich and go to bed. I will clean up down here."

"Thank you so much, Jess. You are the best."

• • • • •

I woke up the next morning at 7:00 a.m., went downstairs to play with and feed my angels, showered, got dressed, and left for the hospital with Jessica. When I got there, Dr. Walden was going into Alfred's room with his chart.

"Good morning, Brenda and Jessica."

"Hi, doctor, how is Alfred? Are these his test results?" I asked.

"Yes, and, unfortunately, the news is not good."

"Tell me, doctor, what is it?"

"The tumors we took out are cancerous, and the cancer has metastasized."

"What does that mean?"

"The fact is the cancer has spread to other parts of the body. There isn't much we can do to control it."

"Can't you give him radiation or chemotherapy?" I asked.

"If we caught it in time, yes, we could have treated the cancer before it spread. But now, all we can do is make him as comfortable as possible, because he will experience a great deal of pain. I am so sorry, Brenda."

"Thank you, doctor," said Jessica. "Brenda, I know this is difficult, but you have to be strong now for you and Alfred because he is going to need you now more than ever."

"I will try." I turned towards the doctor. "Does Alfred know about the results?" I asked.

"No, I was on my way to his room when I saw you."

"Can I be there when you tell him?"

"By all means, right this way."

We all entered Alfred's room. I walked up to his bed and took his hand.

"Hi, honey, how are you feeling?"

"Hello, baby, I am in a little pain, but okay, I guess."

"Hi, Doc. Have the test results come back yet?" Alfred asked.

"Yes, they have."

"Well, what's the damage?"

"Alfred, our tests show the tumors we removed are cancerous and have spread to other parts of your body. I can have you scheduled for chemotherapy and radiation treatments, but due to the fact the cancer is spreading, I'd rather not put your body through the radiation or chemotherapy because, at this point, it would not be effective."

"I would not want to go through the radiation or chemo treatments anyway. How long do I have to live?"

"Alfred, I can't honestly answer that question because I have seen people in your condition live for a few years after being diagnosed, and others maybe six months; it all depends on the individual. You will experience some pain, for which I will prescribe morphine. I want to keep you as comfortable as possible."

"When can I go home, Dr. Walden?"

"Do you think that is a good idea?" asked Brenda.

"I wouldn't recommend you be discharged right now."

"Doctor, what can you do for me here besides give me drugs? I can take morphine at home."

"I see your point. I will discharge you tomorrow afternoon. In the meantime, get some rest."

"Thank you, doctor. Brenda, we have some decisions to make regarding my Will."

"Alfred, we have plenty of time to talk about that."

"Did you hear what the doctor said? I have cancer and I am going to die. I don't have much time left."

"I know it's hard to accept but it is reality, Brenda."

"I just love you so much, Alfred, and I can't live without you."

"I love you more than life too, but we have two beautiful children at home who need to be taken care of, and I want to make sure that happens."

"I know you are right, but I can't help it."

"I want you to call our attorney and have him update my Will, which has you as the beneficiary. Just as before, you will be responsible for my stocks and bonds, real estate, and all of my other financial and business matters. You will never have to work another day in your life. I also have trust funds for Breanna and Alfred Jr., which they will be able to have, once they turn twenty-five years old. Can you please have him draw up the papers for me to sign?"

"Yes, I will call him this afternoon. I feel your parents should know what's going on as well."

"You are right, Brenda, but let me call them. I want it to come from me."

"That's fine, Alfred."

"How are the kids?"

"They are fine. Maria took Breanna to school, and little Alfred is with his play group. I will give them both a big kiss for you."

"Please."

"Alfred, I want to be honest with you. Yesterday, after I left the hospital, I called Jessica and told her what was going on. I know you didn't want anyone to know, but I had to call Jess. Please forgive me."

"Brenda, don't worry, there's nothing to forgive. If I were you, I would have done the same thing."

"I love you so much."

"Where is Jessica now?" he asked.

"In the waiting area."

"Have her come in. I would love to see ole Jess."

I went out into the waiting area where Jessica was chatting with a handsome doctor. I motioned her toward me and she exchanged business cards, then she came to me. I told Jess Alfred wanted to see her, which kind of surprised her, knowing Alfred was a private man.

"Hey, girl, come on in, how are you doing?" he asked.

"I'm okay, more importantly, how are you?"

"I am not doing so well these days, Jess. My time is winding down. I have prostate cancer, which has spread to other parts of my body. It's only a matter of time before my time on Earth is up."

"Alfred, I am so sorry to hear this. It's so unfair. You and Brenda are the best people in the world."

"Thanks, Jess. Stop crying."

"I will try. Is there anything I can do for you?" she asked.

"Yes, as a matter of fact, there is. I would like for you to move up to the main house and stay there with Brenda and the kids permanently. I would feel better knowing you were living with Brenda and the kids and looking out for their well-being."

"I will be more than happy to stay with Brenda and the kids for as long as she needs me."

"Thank you so much, Jess. It's a relief to know you'll be there."

"When are you coming home?"

"First thing tomorrow."

"That's good news."

"I know."

"Honey, you are awfully quiet. Are you alright?" he asked.

"Alfred, I am just trying to process this; everything is happening so fast."

"I understand, Brenda and I are here for you. Jessica, take Brenda home to the kids and I will see you tomorrow morning with my release papers in hand."

"I want to be with you, Alfred."

"Honey, I am in the best of care, and besides, the kids need you, especially now. Give me a big kiss."

"I love you, handsome, and I will see you in the morning," I said.

"Take care, Jess."

"You too, big guy."

• • • • •

As we were driving home, I began crying uncontrollably, which was what I needed to let go and clear my head. All of a sudden, a sense of peace and calmness came over me, as if to say, "Brenda, everything is going to be alright."

"Are you okay, Brenda?" Jess asked.

"Yes, let's go in the house and get things ready for Alfred's homecoming tomorrow."

Breanna and little Alfred met us at the door with big hugs and questions about their father. I gave them the good news that Daddy would be home the next day but he was still sick and needed a lot of rest and care.

"Hello Mrs. Holmes, I have several messages from Alfred's parents for you."

"Thank you, Maria. I should return them; I am sure they have tons of questions for me."

"Brenda, while you do that, I am going to the grocery store. Do you need anything?" Jess asked.

"I'm sure I do. Could you ask Maria? She would know more so than I."

"I will be back in a couple of hours."

I went upstairs to our bedroom, got comfortable, and returned Alfred's parent's call. "Hello, Mr. Holmes, this is Brenda calling."

"Oh, hi, Brenda, how are you doing?"

"I'm hanging in there. Is Mrs. Holmes there? I would like to speak with you both about Alfred."

"She is picking up the extension in the kitchen."

Mrs. Holmes voice appeared on the line. "Hi, Brenda, dear. Alfred called this morning and told us he is in the hospital with prostate cancer that has now spread to other parts of his body. How can this be?"

"Mrs. Holmes, it is just as shocking to me. After I found out Alfred cancelled several doctor's appointments and began to have difficulty urinating, I escorted him to the doctor myself, and that's when we found out that he has cancer."

"But he is so young."

"The doctor said this is common in African American men between the ages of 37-50, and if it's not detected early, it can spread, which in Alfred's case, it has."

"Brenda, can't he undergo chemotherapy?"

"The doctor said, at this stage, it is too late; the chemotherapy would do more harm to his body than good. Right now, all we can do is to keep him as comfortable as possible. Alfred is coming home tomorrow because he wants to spend time with his family."

"Mrs. Holmes and I will be on the next plane," Mr. Holmes interjected.

"Call me with your flight information and I will pick you up at the airport."

"Hang in there, Brenda, we are on our way."

• • • • •

It was comforting to know Alfred's parents would be there, we all needed support from each other. Later in the evening, the hospital called to say Alfred's condition had deteriorated and I should return to the hospital. I ran downstairs, told Maria what was happening, and was off. I arrived at Alfred's room to find him hooked up to several machines. Dr. Walden was going over his chart.

"Doctor, what's going on?" I asked.

"Brenda, Alfred has taken a turn for the worse. His organs are failing and the cancer has spread to his bones."

"How did this happen so fast?"

"Keep in mind the cancer cells have been in Alfred's system for quite some time now."

"I am sorry, you're right. How is he?"

"Alfred is heavily sedated and incoherent."

"I'm staying here with my husband 'til the very end."

"I understand. Is there anything I can do for you, Brenda?"

"Could you please call my house and tell Jessica what's going on? And have her pick up Alfred's parents from the airport."

"Sure."

"Thank you, Dr. Walden."

The doctor left and I sat next to Alfred's bed, holding his hand.

"Sweetheart, Brenda is here."

"Hi, babe. When you married me, I bet you never thought you were getting an old sick man."

"I married a great man, who I love very much. You were the first to make me feel special, wanted, and loved. Who knew back during Freshman Week at Edgar University, we would end up husband and wife?"

"I did," he replied. "Brenda, the first time I laid eyes on you, I knew you were going to be my wife. I want you and our children to enjoy life and be happy because it is so precious. And remember, I will always love and watch over you and the kids."

"Alfred, Alfred, don't leave us. Be strong and hang in there."

"My time is up; it's time for me to leave this earth. Brenda, you are a beautiful and intelligent woman. You have your whole life ahead of you. Promise me, you and the children will be happy."

"Honey, everything will be just fine. Don't worry." Brenda reached over and caressed Alfred's cool body and kissed his blue lips.

At that moment, his parents and sisters entered the room with tears in their eyes.

"Hello son," his father said.

"My baby!" cried his mother.

"Well, Mom and Dad, this is it. I just want to thank you both for being the best parents anyone could hope for. You both have taught me so much about love and life, and I owe all of who I am to you. I love you."

"Son, you made it easy; you made it all easy," said his father.

"We love you so much and we always will," his mother said.

"Take care, love, and enjoy each other," Alfred said.

"Oh, Alfred, this isn't fair. Why you?"

"Don't question why. God doesn't make mistakes, just be happy we had this time together."

Dr. Walden entered the room. "I'm sorry, but Alfred needs his rest now."

"Okay, doctor. We will be right outside," Alfred's father said.

"Doctor, can Brenda stay a while?" Alfred asked.

"Yes, but don't exert yourself; you need your strength."

"Of course, Dr. Walden."

Dr. Walden left the room.

"Alone at last," he said. "Come to bed with me."

"Alfred, is that wise?" I asked.

"I'm sure."

I went to bed, holding the love of my life and asking God to take me and not Alfred. Apparently, God didn't listen to me because the next morning God took Alfred. Telling the children about their dad and planning Alfred's funeral services was the hardest thing I have ever done, and I couldn't have gotten through it without the love and support of my family and my best friend, Jessica.

Alfred's going home service was a wonderful celebration of his life. There were heartfelt and humorous remarks from his friends, family, and colleagues. I know my Alfred was pleased, smiling and saying: "That's my Brenda."

After Alfred's passing, I didn't think I could go on, but, for some reason, Alfred's death was easier to cope with than Robert's. Maybe it was because God had blessed me with two angels to help me through this trying time. When I looked into their innocent eyes, I saw hope and a bright future ahead.

Things were getting back to normal around the house. I was feeding the kids when Jessica came into the kitchen.

"Good morning, Brenda. What's for breakfast? And what's on your agenda for the day?"

"I'm taking the kids to school, and then I'm going to the gym," I replied. "Would you like to join me before going to work?"

"Ha, Ha! Sure, why not? But I'm taking the day off. Brenda, you know you have to get out and stop living just for the kids."

"What do you suggest?" I asked.

"I'm glad you asked, let's start by dropping the kids off. You and I are going to the health spa for a workout, facial, body massage, then off on a shopping spree, and out to lunch. What are you waiting for? Let's go," she continued.

"Jess, can we go eat now? I'm starving."

"Sure, I guess I got carried away."

We left for the spa and went shopping before stopping for something to eat.

"Girl, if you buy another designer suit, I don't know what I'm going to do with you," Brenda teased.

"I love good quality suits."

"Whatever, let's order."

"I am going to have the oriental chicken salad," I said. "What looks good to you, Jess?"

"That distinguished gentleman at the door. He looks very familiar."

"That's Dr. Walden," I said.

"Who?"

"Dr. Walden; he was Alfred's doctor."

"Oh, yeah, he looks yummy without his white doctor's coat on. Brenda, wave him over here and reintroduce me to him."

"Calm down," I said.

"He's looking over this way. Now he's coming over. Do I look hot?"

"Jess, you look wonderful," I said.

"Why, good afternoon, Mrs. Holmes," Dr. Walden said as he approached the table.

"Good day, doctor."

"Please, call me Ian."

"Ian, you remember my friend Jessica."

"Why, yes, it is nice to see you again."

"Ian, would you care to join us?" I asked.

"If it's no trouble."

"No trouble at all," Jess chimed in.

"Brenda, I am glad I ran into you because the hospital needs a new cancer center and at the last board meeting, it was decided to proceed with the project. The members of the hospital board also voted and would like to name the new center in Alfred's name."

"I don't know what to say."

"Alfred would be so proud," said Jess.

"There is one problem: there are some funds available, but we need to raise several million dollars in order to make this center a reality," Dr. Walden explained.

"I know, let's have a gala, a huge ball, where everyone comes out to support a worthy cause. People love to dress up and go out. Brenda, you can head the committee with your marketing and public relations skills," Jess suggested. "And I can crunch the numbers."

"That sounds great, Jessica," he said. "Brenda, what do you think?"

"I'm speechless."

"That means it's a wonderful idea," Jess insisted.

"The board will have their next meeting on Tuesday at 3:00 p.m. Can you both attend?"

"We will be there," I said. "Ian, are you a board member?"

"Yes, and I hope to be working closely with your committee."

"Great."

"I'd love to stay, but I must get back to the hospital."

"Thank you so much, and please, thank the board for me," I exclaimed.

"Sure. We will see you on Tuesday. Enjoy the rest of your day."

"Likewise."

Dr. Walden shook our hands and walked out of the restaurant.

"What a man," Jess sighed.

"Yes, he is very nice."

"Nice? Shit, he is fine!"

"Oh, Jess."

"Let's hurry home and begin brainstorming for this gala. The Alfred Holmes Cancer Center is not going to happen on its own," Jess said.

"Let's go."

· · · · ·

Jessica, Ian, and I worked endless hours planning to make the Alfred Holmes Cancer Center a reality. Jessica was a woman possessed. I knew she really loved Alfred, but I also noticed she had a major crush on the handsome, blue-eyed Dr. Ian Walden. They were always together. It was good to see Jessica happy.

"Brenda, Edgar University's Alumni Association heard about the fundraiser in Alfred's honor and has sent a donation of, get this, four hundred thousand dollars!"

"Oh, my goodness, Jess! Did you say one, two, three, four hundred thousand dollars?"

"Yes I did girl. This is going to be the largest and best fundraiser ever!"

"Alfred would have been so proud," I said.

"Now, if I know Alfred, and I do, he is in heaven watching over us, and orchestrating this entire event."

"I'm surprised Ian isn't glued to your side," I said.

"We have been seeing a lot of each other."

"And?" I asked.

"And I like him very much."

"Have you two?"

"No, we haven't slept together yet, if that's what you are asking?" Jess said.

"Good."

"Ian is special," she said.

"He seems like a nice person. Tell me more about the good doctor."

"If you must know, he is from Martha's Vineyard, Massachusetts. Divorced, no children. He has one sister, and his parents live on the Vineyard, year-round. He completed his undergraduate studies at a university in upstate New York, and he attended medical school in New England."

"That's enough about his career, what kind of person is he?" I asked.

"Oh Brenda, he has an inner beauty, as well as external one. He is in the right profession because he's warm, sensitive, caring, funny, and loves to make one feel special."

"That is great, Jess. The ball is next weekend and everything is in place. If all goes well, we will have raised more than enough money to build the cancer center."

"Brenda, the children will be there, won't they?"

"Yes, as well as Alfred's parents and sisters."

"How are they doing?"

"They're coping."

"I know, more than anyone, how much you loved Alfred. But he has been gone for a year now, and you haven't dated anyone. Girl, you have to move on," Jess said.

"I'm not ready to date again. I'm happy with my family, and besides, I am thinking about starting my career again," I told her.

"Start your career again? You have been out of the game for some time, and from what I've seen, it has changed drastically. Employers are looking for quantity instead of quality. The advertising world has become highly competitive and everyone seems to be under the age of twenty-five."

"Jessica, are you saying I cannot compete in today's market?"

"No, you still have it, girlfriend, don't get me wrong. I'm just saying it is highly competitive in the advertising world these days. Why do you want to go back to work anyway? Alfred left you and the children well taken care of for the rest of your lives."

"It's not about the money, I just enjoy contributing to society and to our community."

"Fine, but couldn't you return to your volunteering with your favorite non-profit organizations by giving X number of hours a week on your own time, let's say, during school hours, which means you would be home after school? Breanna and Al Jr. need you now more than ever, and for you to work full-time would be a great mistake; they would feel totally abandoned."

"Maybe you're right. When did you get to be so smart?" I asked.

"I'm full of surprises, girl."

"Who would have thought in a million years, loose and fancy-free Jessica would be giving me sound advice?" I think someone is finally growing up, and the 'Good Doctor Ian' may have something to do with it," I teased.

"You may have something there, my friend."

Chapter Seven

After the excitement of the ball, things returned to normal. The kids were good, and Jessica was busy with her career and Ian. For the first time since Alfred's death, I felt really alone. I missed Alfred so much.

Sitting at the breakfast bar in the kitchen, sipping my favorite latte and feeling the warmth of the sun beaming through the bay windows, I was taken back to Paris with Alfred where we sat at a local café, sipping on our morning lattes, as the sun came up to greet the day.

While having a beautiful daydream, the telephone rang. Startled, I quickly answered it, hoping it was the wrong number so I could go back to Paris.

"Hello, Brenda sweetheart, this is your mother," the voice said.

My mother always considered me a second-class citizen, and for one reason or another, she didn't visit when I gave birth to her grandchildren. As a child, she told me I would never be productive. And besides, my mother never called me "sweetheart".

"Hello, Mother."

"I hope I haven't taken you away from anything."

"No, just having breakfast."

"Fruit, I hope. The last time I saw you and Jessica, you both were getting a bit chubby," she criticized.

"Thanks for the lovely floral arrangement during my time of bereavement," I said.

"So sorry I could not attend the services; I had a prior commitment in which I could not get out of."

"What was so important you couldn't be with your daughter and grandchildren?"

"Your father was there for you and the kids."

"You mean your grandchildren?"

"Yes, my grandchildren. Brenda, I did not call to argue with you. We have not seen each other in a while and I would like to correct that by coming to visit for a few days, if that's all right with you?" she asked.

"When?"

"I was thinking about flying in on Wednesday morning."

"Fly in? You live only a few hours away."

"Sweetheart, I'm not in Virginia. I'm in Illinois with your brother Stephen and his family at their lovely home."

"Figures," I muttered.

"What was that, dear?"

"Oh, nothing, Mother," I said. "That sounds great. I will meet you at the airport Wednesday morning at ten o'clock."

"I would rather you send a car for me. Your brother did when I arrived in Illinois. Would this put you out in anyway?"

"Mother, there will be a car waiting for you at the airport Wednesday morning."

"Beautiful. And, please, stock the house with my favorite goodies. I will fax you a list as well as my travel itinerary ASAP," she said, hanging the telephone up before I could respond.

"That woman!" I yelled. *Brenda calm down, she's your mother*, I told myself. Needless to say, I couldn't recapture my daydream if my life depended on it.

Before stepping into the shower, I was startled by a hummingbird sound coming from Alfred's study. As I walked toward the mahogany door and turned the knob, there, in the corner of the room, sat the fax machine, spitting out sheets and sheets of paper. As I walked closer to the fax machine, the cover page said:

Facsimile;
To: Brenda Peekson Holmes
From: Mrs. Janice Richardson Peekson
Number of Pages 7

I just spoke with her, what is all of this?

Brenda dear, as per our conversation, here is a list of my must-haves during my visit. You will locate the below items at your specialty and gourmet shops. I hope you can find them.

Regards,
Mother

If I can't find these items, does that mean Mother will stay in Illinois with Stephen? I asked myself. *A list seven pages long of food items for one person. Has she lost it? Let's see what she is requesting.*

Figs
Chocolate Truffles
Pate
Brie Cheese
Artichokes
Real Lobster meat (out of shell)
Octopus in Olive Oil
Gourmet Blueberry Bagels
Crumpets
Scones
Kiwi
Guacamole (fresh)
Freshly ground Amaretto coffee
Mangoes
Four pounds of wild Alaskan salmon

The list went on and on. I wondered how long she planned to visit. And where was my dad? Mother, a woman who was raised on fatback and skillet corncakes, is now requesting pate and mangoes. Go figure.

I took a quick shower, got dressed, and called the area specialty shops to make sure they were fully stocked with Mother's goodies. First stop, the gourmet shop. As I entered the door, the aroma of various imported chesses, meats, and wines filled the air.

"Mrs. Holmes, how nice to see you. You have been away too long. We've missed you. You are one of our favorite customers. How can we help you today?"

"Hello, Mario, it's nice to see you as well. Sorry I haven't been in lately. I'm trying to get things back to normal."

"I was so sorry to hear of Mr. Holmes' passing. He was a good man."

"Thank you, Mario, and thank you, once again, for the delicious food platters."

"It was my pleasure," he said. "What can I do for you today?"

"My mother is coming to visit next week, and here is a list of her favorites."

"No problem, Mrs. Holmes. We will fill this order in no time. Just relax and browse around. We have a recent shipment of your favorite imported wines."

"Thank you, Mario. I will probably need a case of each to get through my mother's visit. Good morning, Mrs. Parker." She was standing right next to me.

"Good morning." She seemed surprised.

"I'm sorry, my name is Brenda Peekson Holmes. I was a teen member at the community center many years ago while you were the executive director."

"Oh, yes, now I remember. How are you? You've grown into a lovely woman, Brenda."

"Thank you, and you are as elegant and youthful as ever."

"You're too kind, and believe it or not, I'm still the executive director but I have relocated to this area."

"Wow! That's wonderful," I said. "Mrs. Parker, how is your family: Neal, Heather, Jennifer, and of course, Mr. Parker?"

"All are doing well. Neal is a corporate attorney in New York City, Jennifer is a CPA with a firm in Dallas, and Heather is a homemaker and mother of two busy and adorable boys, my grandsons; David is five and Matthew is three years old."

"You must be so proud."

"Oh, yes, and yourself?"

"My background is in marketing and advertising. I was a marketing specialist for a major advertising firm for years. I reunited with my college sweetheart, got married and we have two angels; Breanna is nine and Alfred Jr. is five years old. I recently lost my husband to cancer."

"I am sorry to hear of your loss. How are you and the children coping?" she inquired.

"We are all doing well, under the circumstances, with the help of my faith, family, and friends."

"If you ever need to talk about anything, please feel free to call. Here is my card."

"Funny you should mention that, I am currently not working and seem to have a great deal of time on my hands. A friend suggested I volunteer again for a few hours a week with my favorite non-profit organization and I think I just found it at your community center."

"Oh, this is wonderful, Brenda! A person with your background and experience would truly be an asset to the organization."

"Mrs. Holmes, your order is ready," Mario interrupted.

"Don't let me keep you, but as soon as you are up to it, please give me a call," said Mrs. Parker.

"It was lovely to see you again, Mrs. Parker."

"Likewise, Brenda."

It was refreshing to see Mrs. Parker again; she hadn't changed at all. Still as gracious and stunning as ever. If only I could look as stunning at her age.

I glanced at my watch and realized it was late. I sprinted to the car and rushed home to find Jess in my living room, having a sandwich and a glass of mint tea while screaming at the television.

"Hello, Jessica! Please turn the television down or off!"

"Oh, hello, Brenda. I didn't hear you come in."

"How could you with the TV turned up to the highest volume?"

"I'm sorry. Do you need any help with the groceries?" she asked.

"Yes, thanks."

"Are you having a party?"

"I wish. My mother is coming to visit for a few days and she faxed me a list of her favorite foods."

"Sorry to break it to you, but your mother will be here with you for more than a few days; it looks as if she's moving in," she said after looking at the groceries. "What is she coming here for anyway? From what you've told me, she is the black *Mommy Dearest*."

"I really don't know why she's coming to visit now because she wasn't here when I needed her the most."

"Yeah, at Alfred's funeral. Brenda, that's strange."

"I kept making excuses for her absence. So, now that the dust has settled, she decides to visit. Enough about me, how are you and Ian doing?" I asked. "I assume very well, since I haven't seen you in weeks."

"Everything is great. As a matter of fact, Ian and I went to Martha's Vineyard recently."

"Isn't he from there?" I asked.

"Yes."

"And?"

"And I met his parents."

"You go girl! What are they like? Were they nice? Were you nice?"

"Slow down! Everyone was nice. We had a great time. His parents are very warm and receptive people. His mother is a retired second grade teacher, and his father is still a practicing physician. They were very happy to see their son serious about someone for once. Ian's mother and I even made dinner together for our men, even though she did most of the cooking."

"Jess, I am so happy for the both of you."

"He is even talking about settling down and starting a family."

"Are you ready for that?"

"Yes, I am. I can't believe I am saying this."

"I can; when it feels right, you know it. Are we looking at engagement rings yet?"

"No, Brenda."

"Well, once you become engaged, I will give you the biggest and best engagement party this town has ever seen. By the way, while I was in the gourmet shop, I ran into the executive director of the community center, Mrs. Parker. I mentioned to her that I am interested in volunteering at the center."

"What did she say?"

"She was excited and gave me her business card. I will give her a call after my mother leaves."

"Throw that business card away, because your mother is coming to stay."

"HA, HA, HA!"

Chapter Eight

Wednesday morning, the house was immaculate. Maria had really outdone herself. The car had been ordered to pick Mother up from the airport and brunch was in the warmer.

Why am I so nervous? Get a grip, Brenda, it's only your mother, I thought.

The doorbell rang.

"Mrs. Holmes, would you like for me to answer the door?" Maria asked.

"No, thank you Maria, I will get it." I walked slowly to the front door, praying it would be a short but pleasant visit for all concerned. "Mother hello, it's great to see you. How was your flight?"

"Just fine, Brenda. Be a dear and tip the driver."

Brenda, be nice and don't say a word, I said to myself. "Mother, this is Maria Lopez. Maria, this is my mother, Mrs. Janice Peekson. Maria is a Godsend."

"It's nice to meet you, Ms. Lopez."

"Likewise, Mrs. Peekson. I really enjoy working here with your daughter and the children."

"Speaking of the children, when are they expected home?"

"At three o'clock."

"Nice meeting you once again, Mrs. Peekson. Please, let me know if I can do anything to make your stay a pleasant one. Mrs. Holmes, I will be in the kitchen preparing brunch."

"Thank you, Maria."

"Very nice place you have here, Brenda, and a housekeeper as well. Alfred must have left you well off, financially."

"Mother, Alfred and I hired Maria shortly after we were married."

"That's nice, dear."

"Mother, the guest bedroom is located at the top of the stairs, first door on the right, if you would like to freshen up before brunch."

"Great idea; it was a trying flight."

"This evening, we will have dinner with the children on the deck."

"After brunch, I will take a much-needed nap" mother said.

I didn't make an itinerary for my mother's visit. But I planned to take her to all the touristy spots and do some shopping. At three o'clock, the children arrived home from school.

"Mommy, Mommy, we're home!" the kids yelled.

"Hello, my angels! How was school today?"

"Great, Mommy. We're doing fractions and long division in math and it is easy," Breanna said.

"What about you, young man?" I said.

"I'm learning my colors and numbers," little Alfred said.

"That's great. I have two Einsteins in the family."

"Mommy, who is that lady?" Breanna asked.

"Breanna and Alfred Jr., this is my mother and your Grandmother Peekson."

"But we already have a grandmother," Alfred said.

"Honey, you have two grandmothers."

"Come and give your Grandmother Peekson a hug," Mom said.

"Did you bring us presents? Grandmother Holmes always bring us presents when she visits," Breanna stated.

"I didn't think you needed anything," she said.

"And they don't." *But it would have been nice for you to bring something for the children,* I thought. "Go upstairs and get cleaned up for dinner," I told the children. "Mother, is there anything special you'd like to do during your visit with us?"

"No, not really."

"I thought we would go shopping and do some sightseeing."

"Sounds nice," she commented.

"How is Dad and where is he these days?"

"This month he's in Saudi Arabia making his famous oil deals."

"As long as he's happy and safe, that's all that matters," I said.

"True, but he should consider retirement. Brenda, your father's getting up there, and I want the two of us to travel and see the world together with no work involved. I don't want to end up being some lonely old widow."

"Thanks a lot mother."

"I'm sorry, but you know what I'm trying to say," she said.

"Yes, Mother, I know exactly what you're trying to say. As long as Dad is healthy and happy, I feel he should not retire." *Besides, his job keeps him away from you,* I thought.

· · · · ·

During the next several days, I took mother and the children sightseeing and shopping. We went to the aquarium, the zoo, the amusement park, as well as the theater to see a musical play. My mother didn't like the play but the kids loved it.

"Brenda, I can't believe I am leaving tomorrow. These few days just flew by. It's a pity I didn't get a chance to see Jessica during my stay."

"Yes, she had to fly to Dallas unexpectedly. Mother, since this is your last night here, let's pop some popcorn and watch old movies."

"Don't you think you're too old for this slumber party thing?" she said.

"No and it will be fun."

"I am tired, Brenda."

"Just for a little while mother?"

"Thirty minutes," she said. "What movie would you like to see?"

"Surprise me," she said. "Tell me, Mother, what really brought you here to visit me?"

"What do you mean?"

"Well, I haven't exactly been your favorite child and when I needed you the most, you were never around. So, I ask you again, why now?"

"Because I love you."

"You love me? You have a funny way of showing it!"

"Watch your tone, young lady. I am still your mother! Stephen would never speak to me in that tone!"

"He has no reason to. I'm sick and tired of you comparing every goddamn thing I do to your precious Stephen. I'm not Stephen! Nor will I ever be! I don't want to be like Stephen! Ever since I was a little girl, you have been comparing me to Stephen. And when you noticed I had my own mind and made my own decisions, that's when you would constantly tell me "Brenda, you are nothing like your brother. You will never amount to anything. I don't know what to say about you!" Do you know how that made me feel, hearing my own mother say those words to me over and over? How could you do that to your own daughter? The icing on the cake was when you didn't come to visit me when Breanna or Alfred Jr. were born, nor did you come to Alfred's "Going Home" service! You never liked Alfred anyway!"

"That is not true, Brenda!"

"Not true? Not true? Didn't you say Alfred was too dark and didn't come from a suitable family like Morgan?" I asked, becoming angrier.

"I just said you could have done better. And Morgan was very charming," she said.

"Morgan is a cheating, lying asshole who could never love anyone, even himself! But you'd probably love me to be miserable and lonely, wondering where and with whom my husband is sleeping with on any given night! Well, I am sorry to have disappointed you, Mother! All my life you have done nothing but put me down, regardless of my many successes! You didn't win this one, because I am the luckiest and happiest woman alive, and it is due to Alfred, who took me by the hand and accepted me as I am, faults and all! Now that's true love, something you know nothing about!"

I felt a slap across my face, which felt like a million piercing needles.

"Don't you ever speak to me in that tone, young lady!"

"The truth hurts, doesn't it? I have kept this inside of me for years. Enough is enough!"

"I refuse to listen to this nonsense!" she screamed. "I'm going to pack my bags and leave on the first plane out of here!"

"Is that all you have to say, Mother?"

Mother was obviously upset. Her face was bright red and her body was trembling. She didn't say a word as she ran upstairs and slammed the bedroom door.

"That's very mature, Mother!" I shouted from downstairs.

My mother was upset with me and she probably wouldn't speak to me ever again. But this was something I had to do. It had been brewing for years and I had to let her know that her putdowns had affected me, and I'm glad I did.

• • • • •

Saturday morning, the kids were sound asleep. The house was still and peaceful with the aroma of "Mocha Almond" coffee brewing in the kitchen.

God bless Maria; she seems to always know what I need. Then I heard footsteps coming downstairs. I thought it was Mother. What could I say to her? Maybe good morning for starters.

"Maria!"

"I'm sorry if I startled you, Mrs. Holmes."

"That's alright. I just thought you were my mother. Why do you have her bed linen?"

"Your mother is gone; she left last night."

"What?"

"Yes, she told me she was flying back to Virginia. She wanted me to say good-bye for her."

"Oh, really?"

"Yes, ma'am."

"Thank you, Maria."

Why would my mother leave without even saying goodbye to the kids? I don't understand that woman sometimes. Let's hope she will at least call to let me know she arrives home safely.

• • • • •

Maria made the best coffee; not too strong and not too weak, just right. *Where was the remote control?* I thought. Hopefully, I could watch the early edition news before the kids are up and changed the station to their favorite cartoons.

As the pictures came into focus, the anchor said: "This just in: there has been a plane crash at the Hawn Airport. Milbury Airlines, Flight #3064, leaving Hawn Airport, scheduled to arrive in Bloomington, Virginia, crashed shortly after takeoff last night and there are no known survivors. We will pass on more information as it becomes available."

"Oh my God! My mother was on that flight!" I yelled. "Oh my God! Oh my God! What is the Hawn Airport's phone number?" I asked Maria.

"Here it is. Calm down, Brenda."

"Hawn Airport, currently all lines are busy. Stay on the line and your call will be answered in the order it was received," an automated voice responded.

"Someone hurry and answer the phone!" I yelled.

Finally, a representative came on the line. "Hawn Airport, may I help you?"

"Yes, my name is Brenda Holmes and I think my mother was on the flight that crashed last night."

"Just a moment."

Jessica entered the room. "Good morning, girl. What's for breakfast?"

"Jessica, I am glad to see you," I said.

"What's up? Why are you crying?"

"My mother may be dead!"

"What?"

"We had a huge fight last night and she took the first plane home. On the news this morning, they said the flight she was on crashed and there are no survivors! I am on hold with the airport right now."

"Put the telephone down, get dressed, and we'll go to the airport because they won't tell you anything on the phone."

"You're right. I'll be two minutes. Maria, Jess and I are going out for a while. Feed the children and we will check in later."

"Of course."

"Let's go, Jess," I said.

As Jessica was speeding down the expressway to the airport, I said while crying, "This is all my fault."

"What do you mean?" Jess asked. "You have no control over what happens on an airplane."

"It's my fault my mother took this flight. If I didn't open my mouth but she has been a controlling *Mommy Dearest* for most of my life."

"Well, yes Brenda, and it is not your fault."

"I should call Dad."

"Don't get ahead of yourself, Brenda. Let's see what's what before calling anyone."

The parking lot was filled with television trucks and crews from across the state, but luckily, we found a parking spot near the entrance.

"What now, Jess? There are so many people here."

"There's an information desk."

We walked over to the attendant. "Hello, my name is Brenda Peekson Holmes and my mother may have been on the flight which crashed last night."

"Just a moment, Ms. Peekson Holmes, we are trying to accommodate all family members. Please have a seat in room 514 with the other family members until further notice."

"Okay, thank you."

"Brenda, have a seat and try to relax. Can I get you something?" Jess asked.

"Some water would be nice."

"Water it is."

"Thanks."

"It's not fair to have family members waiting with no information of what's going on."

"No news is good news, Brenda."

"Just try to stay positive. I know it's hard, because you have several emotions going on inside, but whatever happens, we will get through it together."

Finally, the door opened and several distinguished men of authority in navy-blue suits, with clipboards in hand, entered the room. "Good morning ladies and gentlemen, my name is Mr. Bradley Gowan, the Public Information Director for Milbury Airlines. There has been a fatal accident on Milbury Airlines Flight #3064, leaving Hawn Airport, destination, Bloomington, Virginia. Unfortunately, there are no known survivors on this flight. I have a list of passenger names on this flight, and will read them in alphabetical order."

As Mr. Gowan began reading the names, I shook, and Jessica held me as tight as she could. I was in another world; I heard faint outbursts in the background as people heard the names of their loved ones being read. Finally, Mr. Gowan came to the last name on the list. "Jeremey Zippa."

"Brenda, Brenda, your mother's name was not called! She was not on that flight!"

"Really?" I asked.

"Yes, really, Brenda."

"Well, where could she be?" I went up to Mr. Gowan. "Excuse me, Mr. Gowan."

"Yes"

"My mother, Mrs. Janice Peekson, was scheduled to be on this flight, but her name was not called."

"Well, this is the list of all passengers who were on flight #3064."

"Where can she be? This not knowing is driving me crazy."

"Brenda, let's go back to the information desk and have her paged," Jess suggested.

"May I have your attention please, Mrs. Janice Richardson Peekson, will you please report to the information desk ASAP!"

"Thank you again," I said.

"Brenda, I do believe you are getting on this woman's last nerve."

"I can't help it; my mother is missing."

"I'm sorry Brenda. We will find her."

"Let's have a seat and talk about something else for a while," I said.

"Have you started volunteering with the community center yet?" Jess inquired.

"No, I planned to give Mrs. Parker a call next week."

"Do you have any ideas regarding fundraising projects?"

"I really haven't had time to think about it, but a few things come to mind."

"Such as?"

"A sock hop, a seventies dance night, a silent auction, and maybe a golf tournament, where local businesses could sponsor the events."

"That's my girl."

"I still have it."

"You never lost it, girl."

"Thanks, Jess."

"For what?"

"For being the best friend anyone could possibly hope to have."

"No problem. I love you. You know what, Brenda? Your mom could have taken another flight."

"You're right. How can we find out?"

"There is Mr. Gowan again. Let's ask him."

Mr. Gowan suggested we go to any Millbury Airlines Customer Service desk and they should be more than happy to assist us.

"Come on, Jessica!"

"I'm coming, I'm coming!" Jess said.

As we approached another information desk, Jessica spoke on my behalf. "Hello, we would like some information regarding one of your passengers. Is there a woman by the name of Mrs. Janice Richardson Peekson leaving the Hawn Airport for Bloomington, Virginia, booked to fly out anytime today or last night?"

"Let me see…Mrs. Janice Richardson Peekson. No, no, I don't have anyone by that name on any flight going to any part of Virginia, ma'am."

"Are you sure?"

"Yes, I am."

"Thanks anyway."

"This doesn't make any sense. She left the house in the middle of the night and told Maria she was going home. Where can she be? Should I call the police?" I asked.

"Slow down, let's not panic. Think for a minute. Let's sit over here at Gate 7 and put our heads together before calling in the National Guard. Okay, does your mother know anyone in town besides you?"

"No."

"Are you sure?"

"I'm positive."

"Not changing the subject or anything, but that's a nice set of designer luggage sitting over there all alone on the floor. The owner must be very rich or very stupid," Jess commented.

"Wait, it looks like my mother's limited edition set of designer luggage!"

"Go and see."

"Yes. It even has her initials on it!"

"Brenda, this is good news; this means she must still be here!"

"Let's go back to the information desk and have her paged again."

"Don't leave the luggage." Jess said. We returned to the desk. "Hi, we hate to bother you again, but could you please page Mrs. Janice Richardson Peekson throughout the airport several times?"

"Of course. Mrs. Janice Richardson Peekson, will you please dial 411 to the information desk immediately."

"Brenda, she will hear the page, dial 411, and we will find her location."

"Why hasn't she called yet? What is taking so long?" I asked.

"It's only been a few minutes," Jess reassured me. "Look Brenda! As hot as it is, that woman is wearing a mink coat."

"That's my mother!"

"Mother! Mother!" I shouted as I ran through the airport like I was in one of those rental car commercials.

"Brenda, what are you doing here?" she asked.

"Oh Mother, I am so happy to see you, and I love you! I thought you were on the plane that crashed, because Maria said you were flying out last night on that flight. It was my fault you left the house upset, and if anything were to happen to you, I would never forgive myself."

Mother noticed Jessica for the first time. "Hello, Jessica," she said in a cool manner.

"Hi Mrs. Richardson Peekson, I'm so happy you are okay. Why don't you two have a seat in one of the conference rooms for more privacy? I will make a few phone calls and guard your luggage with my life, Mrs. Richardson Peekson" Jess said.

As we made ourselves comfortable in the conference room, I asked, "Mother, why did you leave last night without saying goodbye?"

"I was very hurt and upset last night, and, at the time, I thought it best for all that I left before anymore was said. My plan was to hop on the next plane out of here, but I thought it would be better if I cooled down and thought about what was said. So, I went to the airport hotel and booked a room for the night. I was going to call you tonight to apologize."

"No, Mother, I should apologize to you."

"No, what you said last night made a great deal of sense. I should thank you for being strong enough to tell me how you felt," she replied. "I know I haven't been the kind of mother you would have wanted, but, with your father on the road ten months out of the year, I was left to raise six children the only way I was taught. Brenda, I have made many mistakes along the way, but I am going to break the cycle, starting today. I want to renew our mother/daughter relationship. Going forward, I will be more considerate, caring, understanding, and will remember that all my children are individuals, with their own ideas, goals, and choices, and I should respect them. And most of all, I promise to listen to you, as well as the rest of my family. I have realized today, more than ever, you don't always get a second chance and I have."

"I am blessed."